THE ONE SAFE PLACE

Tania Unsworth

ALGONQUIN YOUNG READERS 2015

For Oscar, whom I love the most,
and Joe Ridley, my favorite

Published by
Algonquin Young Readers
an imprint of Algonquin Books of Chapel Hill
Post Office Box 2225
Chapel Hill, North Carolina 27515-2225

a division of
Workman Publishing
225 Varick Street
New York, New York 10014

First paperback edition, Algonquin Young Readers, May 2015.
Originally published in hardcover by Algonquin Young Readers, April 2014.
Printed in the United States of America.
Published simultaneously in Canada by
Thomas Allen & Son Limited.
Design by Carla Weise.

LIBRARY OF CONGRESS
CATALOGING-IN-PUBLICATION DATA
Unsworth, Tania.
The one safe place : a novel / by Tania Unsworth.—First edition.
pages cm
Summary: In a near future world of heat, greed, and
hunger, Devin earns a coveted spot in a home for abandoned
children that promises unlimited food and toys and the hope of
finding a new family, but Devin discovers the home's horrific true
mission when he investigates its intimidating Administrator
and the zombie-like sickness that afflicts some children.
ISBN 978-1-61620-329-0 (HC)
[1. Abandoned children—Fiction. 2. Orphans—Fiction.
3. Survival—Fiction. 4. Science fiction.] I. Title.
PZ7.U44178On 2014
[Fic]—dc23   2013043145

ISBN 978-1-61620-483-9 (PB)

10 9 8 7 6 5 4 3 2 1
First Paperback Edition

THE ONE SAFE PLACE

One

I<small>T WAS THREE O'CLOCK</small> in the afternoon before Devin was done digging the grave. He had really finished it at two, but had carried on for an hour longer, partly to make sure it was good and deep and partly to delay what was coming next. He stood in the bottom of it, resting. The hole was higher than his waist; a rectangle with uneven sides. Devin would have liked to straighten it out. It was too broken up and prickly. But it was the best that he could do.

He threw the shovel over the side of the grave and hauled himself out. There was a slight breeze at the top of the hill, and he stood for a few moments looking out over the valley. In the land beyond, his grandfather had told him, there had once been corn. They used to farm it with machines as wide as houses and it poured like gold, rushing and endless, into vast granaries.

That was more than fifty years ago, before it got hot. It hardly ever rained now except for massive storms that darkened the skies for days. Huge areas of land had become useless, the dry soil swept away by the wind or by sudden, treacherous floods that ripped everything in their path. The change in the weather had started slow, but then it had come fast, faster than anyone expected. But it wasn't just the weather that had changed, his grandfather said. It was people too. People had scattered. They lost homes and livelihoods, and desperation had turned their hearts as hard as the parched earth itself.

It was different on their small farm. The land was still good, a pocket of richness.

"We're lucky, then," Devin had said.

"We're fortunate," his grandfather corrected him.

It was important, his grandfather said, to keep to the right meanings of words or else they would be lost; blown away like the soil that had once grown enough corn to feed a nation. Other things also needed to be kept. Manners at table, the shine on the old silver vase. Every day, his grandfather fetched one of their books so Devin could practice his reading. They had five books. One was about farming, how to grow things and raise animals, and one was full of stories with no pictures except the ones the words made in your head. Another one had nothing but pictures, images of people who were dead now and places that were far away, and animals so strange they made Devin laugh.

"No," his grandfather said when Devin stumbled over his reading. "That's an *a*, not an *e*."

"But they're so hard to tell apart," Devin complained. "Both so pale they fade into the page . . . and they won't stop chirping, Granddad."

"Chirping?"

"Like the swallows," Devin explained.

When his grandfather smiled, his lips barely moved, as if his smile was another thing to be kept, guarded from view like a treasure. Instead you saw it mostly in his eyes. He reached out and touched Devin's hand, and the taste on Devin's tongue was half earthy, half sweet, like roots that had grown to fullness beneath the dark ground.

"Try again, Dev. Try again, my lad."

Devin hadn't thought his grandfather was old. He'd thought he was strong, as strong as the barn and the hills. He could labor all day until his shirt was wet through, but he'd never take it off and work naked to the waist because that was yet another thing to be kept: your standards. You had to keep your standards, he said, in such a shifting world. Since he'd been a boy, there'd been a thousand new inventions. You could do almost everything now just with the push of a button. But nothing had solved the problem of the heat, or the greed and hunger that had followed.

"Why not?" Devin had once asked.

His grandfather had squinted up into the blazing sun and pursed his lips.

"Nobody thought about the future, I guess. Too busy with other things."

✦ ✦ ✦

Devin couldn't delay any longer. He picked up the shovel and turned back down the hill, toward the farmhouse. The basket of apples was still there where he'd dropped it, the fruit scattered all over the yard. His grandfather was still there too, lying on the porch with his eyes wide open and his long arms flung out. For half a second Devin thought he saw the fingers of one hand move and he scrambled up the stairs, falling to his knees as he grabbed for it.

But the hand was as cold as ice.

Tears of grief and panic rose in Devin's eyes. But he couldn't cry. There was nobody left to be strong except for him. He shoved his palms into his eyes, pressing back the tears.

"I dug it the best I could," he told his grandfather. "It's good and deep. The coyotes won't find you. You'll be safe."

Devin stayed by his grandfather's side for a long while. The shadows were growing long when he finally rose to his feet. He went into the bedroom and took the sheet off the bed and spread it wide and white on the porch. Then he half pushed, half rolled his grandfather onto it, his hands shaking and his breath coming fast. His horse, Glancer, named for her shy, sideways look, nickered softly from the orchard, and Devin hesitated. Then he covered his grandfather with the sheet and began to sew the sides together as quickly as he could.

When he was finished, he fetched Glancer, hitched her to the low wagon and brought her round to the front of the house. His grandfather's heels banged on the porch stairs as Devin dragged him down, and each thud was like a blow to his heart. It took a long time to get the body into the wagon, but at last it was done and Devin slowly led Glancer up the hill, taking the shovel with him.

✦ ✦ ✦

It was nearly dark and his grandfather was just a dim shape at the bottom of the grave, the sheet covering him as pale as the wing of a moth. After the struggle to move the body, Devin thought filling in the grave with earth would be easy. But it wasn't. It felt like the hardest thing he had ever had to do. He stood holding the first shovelful of dirt, unable to move.

Burying his grandfather felt so final. And when it was done, he would be quite alone.

Although it was late, it was still hot. Devin put down

the shovel and wiped the sweat from his face, catching the scent of rosemary on his fingers. It made a long, sighing sound, and a flash of blue, very bright and clean, shot for a second behind his eyes. The herb grew wild here on the top of the hill. Devin's grandfather had pointed out the wiry plants, explaining that rosemary was the toughest of herbs, able to survive almost anywhere.

"Smells good, doesn't it?" He'd held out a sprig for Devin to sniff. "A long time ago, people used to place it in graves for remembrance."

Devin turned away now, searching in the gloom for the familiar plant. He found a bush and tugged a small branch free. For a second or two, he held it to his face, breathing in the scent, and then he tossed it into the grave and began shoveling in dirt as quickly as he could. "I'm sorry," he told his grandfather. "I love you, I'm sorry." He was crying now, his tears mingling with the dusty clods.

"I won't forget you. I never will, no matter what."

When the grave was all filled in, Devin collected rocks and placed them in a circle on top. Circles rang clear and they were always gold.

"Like the corn," he told his grandfather. "Remember you told me you saw it? When you were a boy?"

It was a comfort knowing he could talk to his grandfather, even though he was dead. And if he closed his eyes, he could even imagine that his grandfather was talking right back to him.

But that night, alone in his bed, he couldn't imagine his grandfather saying anything at all.

Devin woke before dawn and rose to do his chores. The chickens had to be fed and the wood collected and the cow watered and led out into the little field. He went as fast as he could, the bucket of water from the spring banging painfully against his shins as he stumbled across the yard.

The hay needed to be cut. It normally took him and his grandfather a full day and a half. Devin fetched his scythe and stood still for a moment, staring at the meadow. It suddenly seemed enormous. But he bent his head and set to work, not knowing what else to do, his arms moving automatically. By midday his hands were blistered and his breath was ragged with panic.

The grass was barely a quarter cut.

Leave a job undone, his grandfather always said, and it will just get bigger.

But Glancer's stall needed to be cleaned out and the vegetable patch weeded, and the apples were still lying in the orchard . . . Devin worked all day and into the night, every hour a little further behind.

Midnight found him setting traps in the field for rabbits, his fingers trembling with fatigue. What if he actually caught one? What then? He had never killed a rabbit before. His grandfather always did it, his big hands quick and merciful. Devin had grown a lot in the last year, but there were still many things he couldn't do.

His grandfather had gone before he could teach Devin everything. Perhaps like everyone else, his grandfather hadn't thought enough about the future. He had been too busy with other things. Devin dropped his head and wept, too exhausted even to wipe his face.

The next day was worse than the one before, because his grandfather was right, jobs left undone just grew bigger and bigger. He ate the last of the cornbread and some raw carrots; there was nothing warm to eat because he hadn't had time to fill the stove and light it. Despair began to creep over him.

He lay on his bed that night with his boots still on and his hands and face unwashed. A great silence came. It swept through the orchard and over the fields and trickled along all the veins and tunnels in his body, right into his fingers. He looked up through the window at the stars, but even they made no noise.

In the morning Devin got up and gathered provisions: boiled eggs, vegetables, a knife, his grandmother's locket, and the small handful of coins from the pot in the kitchen. The city was far to the north. His grandfather used to live there years ago and had described it to him—the buildings, the huge numbers of people. Devin had trouble imagining crowds. He visualized himself and his grandfather and then added all the people from the picture book. It came to about fifty or sixty, which seemed like an impossibly large number.

"You'll go there someday too, Dev," his grandfather had told him. "When you're ready to leave."

"When will I be ready to leave?"

"When you know for sure how to come back again."

Devin didn't think that time had come. He didn't feel ready at all. But in the city he would find help, someone to work on the farm, perhaps. He couldn't do it alone, and the longer he waited, the more impossible it would become.

He went to the spring and filled up the large leather water carrier. Then he opened the gate to the field so the cow could roam free. There was nothing he could do for the chickens, but they were hardy creatures and he thought most would survive until he got back. Finally Devin went to the barn and led Glancer out. He took off her halter and stood for a long moment with his forehead resting against her nose, feeling her breath, the shiver of her skin. She had been his horse since before he could remember, and the beating of her heart was as familiar as his own.

"Go," he whispered at last. "I can't take you. Go."

The horse stood in front of the barn, not moving as Devin walked away, but when he looked back a moment or two later, she had already wandered off a little way, head down, her brown rump shadowed by the trees. From behind the barn, the rooster crowed purple and then fell silent.

Devin turned toward the north and began to walk.

Two

THE CITY WASN'T ANYTHING like his grandfather had described. It was more like something out of a nightmare.

It had taken Devin a week of walking over hard and desperate country to reach it. His farm lay in a tiny valley watered by a secret spring that flowed into a stream. Millions of years ago, the earth itself had slipped and formed this hidden place, surrounded on all sides by slopes of rock. The only way in or out of the valley was a narrow path that twisted between immense boulders. If you didn't know the valley was there, you would miss it completely. Inside, sheltered from the worst of the sun, there were trees and fields and meadows.

Outside it was different.

Outside it was dry and flat and empty. The earth had a weightless feel, rising in small clouds of dust as Devin trudged along, the water carrier bouncing at his waist, his eyes pinched against the glare of the sun. He stumbled over slopes of loose white stones, his feet slipping, sending the stones skittering and bouncing. Ahead lay a huge expanse where little grew except low, brittle shrubs the same color as the earth. The sky seemed far higher than normal, as if someone had scraped away at the underside of it, leaving nothing but a thin, burning shell. Eventually Devin came to a channel in the ground and clambered down into it. It was an old, dried-up riverbed. He could see where water had once smoothed and hollowed out the rocks.

On the second day, Devin saw the biggest coyote he'd ever seen in his life. It trotted across his path, ignoring him, its muscles moving like liquid beneath its hide. During the afternoon of the third day he saw buildings.

At first he thought he must have arrived at the city, because there were so many buildings; he counted nearly a hundred. From a distance everything looked orderly, almost neat; but as he approached, he saw tilting roofs and weeds creeping out through cracks in the sidewalks. Devin walked down a broad street with homes on either side. Drifts of dust had gathered on the doorsteps like silent visitors, and children's toys lay scattered in the backyards. Ragged clothes hung from a broken washing line. A row of poplar trees had been planted on the edge of town but they were brown and dead.

There was nobody around. They must have left a long time ago, Devin thought. And they had gone without picking up the toys or taking in the laundry, as if they knew they weren't ever coming back.

There was a main street, with bigger buildings, some with large glass windows so you could look inside, but there was nothing to see except some bottles smothered with cobwebs, and rows of empty shelves. There was a car parked on the street, its lid open. Devin knew it was a car because he had seen pictures of them. They didn't have a car at the farm, nor any machines or artificial lighting or screens or buttons, nothing that his grandfather called technology. It was foolish to rely on such things, his grandfather had said, because if they went wrong, you were stuck. You were better off relying on yourself.

Devin peered under the lid of the car and saw a mass of wires and dirt. It was hard to imagine that this battered old thing had ever moved. He reached up and closed the lid, not sure why he was doing it, only that it felt a little terrible to leave it gaping open like that.

The next day he came to a road. It was the straightest and flattest thing he'd ever seen in his life. Vehicles were moving along it, although they looked different from the car in the abandoned town. These were low to the ground and made no more sound than a whisper as they passed by, shrinking to dots on the horizon. They must be some of the new inventions his grandfather had talked about, Devin thought. He tried to see who was driving them, but he could sense only dim shapes inside. For a second he thought of trying to stop one, but he was frightened by their strangeness and their speed. How did people breathe, traveling so fast? Just looking at them made him dizzy.

Soon after, he ran out of water. He found a spot where more shrubs grew and began to dig, as his grandfather had taught him. He dug with his hands and then with a sharp stick; the hole was deep before he finally saw a thin layer of liquid seeping up through the gravel. He took off his shirt and wet it and squeezed it carefully into his carrier. The water amounted to barely half a cup, and it tasted orange-brown and gritty.

On he went, a lonely speck against the sky. More roads appeared, forking in various directions. Then on the seventh day he came to hills, empty at first but becoming greener. Plants meant water, he thought. Perhaps he was on the outskirts of the city at last.

To begin with, it seemed like a pleasant place, although strange. There were a great many trees. They weren't the trees he was used to but tidy things, regularly separated, their trunks surrounded by tiny fences. Then a large green space opened up. At first Devin took it for cloth, but then he saw it was grass, although unlike any that he had ever seen before. It was cut perfectly evenly and very close to the ground, but what astonished him most was the color—a green of such tingling, glassy richness that he immediately sank to his knees to examine it further. The ground was moist, although no rain had fallen in many days. Devin thought perhaps it was watered by underground streams or pipes, although why anyone would go to that trouble for mere grass, clearly not intended for the grazing of livestock, he didn't know.

A little farther along, he came upon houses. They were huge, the size of three barns, and they were surrounded by more of the strange grass, and their roofs were covered with great shining panels of something that looked like glass, only darker. The houses were all completely spotless. Even the borders of the flower beds were razor sharp.

Every single house was set back and every single one was surrounded by steel fences.

As he stared, the windows in one house seemed to move, the horizontal shutters gliding closed like eyes blinking shut. But he didn't see any people at all. It was very quiet.

A few cars passed him. They were larger than those he'd seen on the highway and had windows that weren't clear glass, but darkened to a whistling brown so that he couldn't see inside at all.

The city looked to be almost empty, Devin thought. But then, coming around a corner to the top of the highest hill, Devin saw he was completely wrong about this. These houses, these gates and pathways and stretches of perfect grass, were only a corner of the city, a tiny section, sheltered by trees. The rest of it—the real city—lay below him.

It was a vast jumble of buildings, one on top of the other, dusty and crowded. Some of the buildings looked half in ruins; others had huge pictures flickering on them. Great flocks of birds wheeled and darted overhead. In the middle of the confusion lay the thick brown stripe of a river, the water flowing low and sluggish around the legs of three great bridges that rose with a tangled arrangement of pillars and cables. A yellow haze obscured the farther horizon, and Devin heard a distant roar, made up of a million voices.

For a second, his courage failed him and he thought of turning back. But he was very tired and there was nowhere else to go.

✦ ✦ ✦

Devin made his way through a labyrinth of streets and found an alley as the sky grew dark. He curled up in a pile of dirty paper, his hands clutched tight against his chest. At dawn three boys, older than he was and far stronger, attacked him, keeping him face down on the ground while they searched his clothes. In three minutes they had taken everything: his knife, jacket, coins, the last of his food, and even his boots. They didn't find his grandmother's locket, because Devin had hidden it in the hem of one of his pant legs. He lay on the ground after they'd gone, too terrified to move for several minutes. Then he got to his feet and limped to the entrance of the alley.

He was in a street so crammed with people that he almost bumped into a woman walking past, leading a small child by the hand.

"Please," Devin said, his voice jerky with shock. "Please, they took everything. Can you help me?"

The woman looked at him quickly and her mouth went tight and her eyes swung away. She shook her head with a small, angry gesture and hurried on, pulling her child with her. A boy riding a two-wheeled vehicle with a huge box on the back swerved suddenly out of the crowd toward him. Devin stumbled back and half fell. "Need help?" the boy shouted in a laughing voice. "Call the POLICE! Ha!" And then he was gone, as quickly as he came.

Nobody else seemed to have noticed. Everyone was moving, jostling, hurrying. Most of the buildings nearby were run down, and the ground was littered with trash and pieces of brick. Devin joined the stream of people, not knowing what else to do.

He began to walk fast and then broke into a trot. The wide street met another, and then a huge crossroads of four streets met in a knot of dust and traffic. There were more two-wheeled things, and small, old-looking cars, and men dragging light carts as they ran along. So many people, faces upon faces. Devin whirled and ducked, unable to take it all in; the clamor and color, the flapping clothes and spinning wheels, the market stalls, the doors and dark openings, the noise of a thousand things clanging and clattering.

He was running now, his bare feet hot against the broken sidewalk, his skin burning with a hundred sensations at once, his ears ringing painfully, his head pounding. At last he stopped and crawled under a sheet of corrugated iron that was leaning against a wall. He crouched there for a long time, watching feet pass in front of his shelter, his hands pressed tight to his ears, his mind grappling with the reality that faced him.

His idea to get help with the farm had seemed simple when he was back home. Now that he was in the city, it was a different matter. He couldn't just go up to someone and ask. He might have if there had been three—or five—or even ten people here. But there were so many. He had no idea where to begin or whom to approach. You had to know people, he thought. Or else they would look at you like the woman with the child had. Or not look at you at all.

Devin was very hungry. He crept out from his hiding place and began to search for food. He scavenged scraps from vegetable stalls and bins, trudging the streets as the hours passed. Water was scarce. There were long lines of people waiting for their turn at a single faucet, and it ran out before he got anywhere near the front. He didn't understand why there was so little water when he had seen such green grass in the other part of the city, the area with the big houses.

He noticed other things too. Like the huge, new cars that sometimes appeared amid the old, ramshackle vehicles. Or the man he saw get out of one such car with shoes that shone and glasses that were black and a strange device attached to the side of his head that he seemed to be talking into. Or the tall building, covered with glass so clean and bright that it looked as if it had descended from the sky to land among the tatty, broken-down buildings around it. These things didn't look as if they belonged. Or perhaps it was the rest of the city that didn't belong. It confused Devin, although nobody else around him seemed to notice. The man who got out of the car, for instance, hadn't appeared to see a ragged old lady with bare feet sitting only a little way away on the sidewalk.

The whole place seemed lopsided, Devin thought. Out of shape and out of balance.

A little later, Devin spotted a man lying in the street as if he were very ill, perhaps even dead. But everyone was simply passing by. One lady actually stepped over the man's body as if it were invisible.

In the afternoon he came to a large, grimy-looking building. There was a word written above the main entrance: POLICE.

That was the word the boy had shouted. Devin stopped. The letter E had slipped a bit and was tilted to the right so that it made the wrong sound, more of a stutter than a chirp. Devin hesitated. He didn't know what the word meant or whether the boy had been right about getting help there. As he watched, a man came out and stood in the doorway. He was large and sweaty and his face was heavy with boredom. He glanced up and saw Devin and his eyes were suddenly hard and threatening and Devin was afraid. He ducked away and hurried down the street, his heart pounding.

His plan to ask someone to come back and cut his hay and patch his barn and help him trap hares seemed stupid now.

When darkness fell, he found his way back to the corrugated-iron shelter and tried to sleep. Even though it was night, the city remained alive with noise, but Devin could still hear the silence. It had followed him all the way from the farm, and now it was here in the city. He could feel it in the pit of his belly and all the way up to his chest.

It was the silence of knowing he was utterly alone.

✦ ✦ ✦

After a day or two, Devin became less fearful and more used to the hubbub of the streets. It was easy to make a

pattern of the place in his mind. The shapes of the buildings sang a song, just like the stones in the old wall that
circled the farm had done, and the colors around him
wove themselves into a fabric as clear as any map.

But the silence never left him.

Nor did his hunger.

He was hungry when he woke up in the morning
and hungry when he went to sleep; and all the time in
between, he spent looking for food. He ate anything he
could find. Scraps of bread, rotten fruit, a handful of
potato peelings flung into the street. He had to be quick
because there were always other people as hungry as he
was. Many of them were children.

The children were all ragged and thin, and they kept
their eyes on the ground, hunting for shreds to eat. It
didn't seem as though anybody was looking after them.
Perhaps there were simply too many children, Devin
thought, and in this strange, lopsided world, nobody
cared about them very much. Not the way his grandfather had cared about him. The other kids didn't speak
to Devin. They didn't even look at him. The silence inside Devin grew until his whole body seemed to ache.

On his third day a girl caught his eye. She was delicate, with dirty reddish hair and pale skin speckled like
an egg. What made him notice her was that she was the
only person he had seen since arriving in the city who
was actually looking up. She walked along slowly, her

gaze fixed on some point along the rooftops. Then she turned a corner and was gone.

A day later, he saw her again. She was crouching alone in the middle of a large area between buildings, in an expanse of broken concrete and stunted weeds. Devin walked closer. The girl looked as if she was hunting for something, her fingers digging through a small pile of rubble. She was so intent on her task that she didn't notice when Devin came right up in front of her.

"What are you doing?"

The girl startled and got to her feet instantly. Her eyes were small and brown and showed no expression. Something glittered in her hand.

"What have you found?"

She didn't reply. Instead she simply turned her back and began to walk away. Inside Devin, the silence surged and pushed until it felt as though it would break the banks of his skin and carry him far away.

"Please!" he cried out. "Please talk to me! Somebody has to talk to me!"

Three

THE GIRL TURNED AROUND. She looked a little younger than Devin, about ten or eleven, although it was hard to tell because she was so slight. Up close, her face was even more covered with freckles than he'd first thought, and her hair was very long and matted. It was tied back with a piece of ribbon that was so chewy pink and crackling that it made him want to smile. She was too wild and odd-looking ever to be called pretty, he thought. But somehow, she was beautiful. She was the most beautiful person he had ever seen in his life.

She opened her hand and showed him what she was holding. It was a sharp piece of something that glimmered with iridescence. She tilted it one way and then another, and where it caught the light it made a line of rainbow so sharp it almost hurt the eye.

"I collect them," she said. "They're just bits. I've never found a whole one. Once I found half. They're mostly buried. You have to look."

"What are they?"

"Discs," she told him. "People used to use them to store information."

Devin had no idea what she was talking about.

"There's pieces of them lying around all over the place," she said.

Devin reached out and took the fragment. The rainbow shimmered with icy prickles that ran down the back of his neck. "It's strange . . . ," he said slowly. "I never felt anything like that before."

The girl nodded. "Well," she said. "Okay. So I answered your question."

She turned and began to walk away. Devin watched her as she went. "Hey!" he called. "You forgot your piece of disc! Hey!" She didn't turn. Without thinking of anything except that he couldn't let her out of his sight, Devin took off running after her.

The girl didn't slow down. When Devin reached her she gave him a quick look and then picked up her pace. She ran lightly, almost effortlessly, her knot of red hair bouncing against the nape of her neck. Soon she was running so fast that she was almost flying, dodging pedestrians, swerving this way and that to avoid obstacles, with Devin keeping pace beside her. They ran through crowded streets, down a long alley, and across an area of wasteland strewn with concrete blocks. At last she stopped.

They were standing in the shadow of a tall building perhaps eight or nine stories high. It looked as if it had been in a fire—one wall was entirely blackened—and the whole thing still smelled of soot. At one point, some-one must have tried to repair the place, because there was scaffolding all the way up to the top. But the effort had clearly been abandoned. Through a broken window, Devin caught a glimpse of a dark and hollow interior.

"Can you climb?" the girl asked.

Devin bent at the waist, panting. "Sure," he said, thinking of the apple trees in the orchard.

But the girl hadn't waited for his answer. She had already swung herself up to the first rung of the scaf-folding and was reaching for the second. Soon she was twenty feet above him. Devin followed. The scaffold-ing creaked and shifted under his weight, and he had to half jump to reach each handhold, his heart pounding. Halfway up he made the mistake of looking down and saw the earth tilt and shimmer in the heat. He stopped, terrified, the stink of the burned building filling his nos-trils, his hands slippery and shaking. He looked up. The girl was already at the top. He saw her head appear over the edge.

"The last part is easier," she said. "Go to the left . . . grab that pole . . . that's it."

Devin took a deep breath and hauled himself up the last stretch. At the top he lay for a second or two without lifting his head, trying to get his breath back. Slowly he got to his feet. They were on the roof. A faint breeze lifted his hair and cooled his face. Below him and stretching all the way to the horizon was the city, shrouded in a golden veil of haze and dust. In the far distance, he could see the hills and woods he had traveled through all those days before, and nearer, the brown stripe of the river and the bridges, tiny from this distance, like things made out of matchsticks. But it wasn't this that made him draw in his breath and stare. It was the roof itself.

The girl had arranged boxes to sit on and an old mattress, covered with a faded sheet. Above it was a canopy, propped up on sticks, a shimmery piece of pale green fabric that fluttered slightly in the wind. All around lay boxes and containers filled to the brim with colored scraps that glittered when they caught the sun. To one side, there was a kind of washing line, a string stretched between two corners of the roof. From the line hung many more of the disc pieces. They glimmered and twisted, flavoring the breeze with the sound of far-off bells.

Devin turned and looked at the girl. She was standing with her arms folded, staring at him.

"If you tell anyone about this place, I'll kill you."

He nodded. "My name's Dev," he said. "It's short for Devin."

"Kit," the girl said.

"What's that short for?"

"Nothing. It beats being called 'kid.' That's all."

Devin frowned. A great tiredness came over him. He went to the mattress and sat down on it. It was quiet up here, but it was a different kind of silence from the one that had followed him from the farm. Above his head, the canopy fluttered gently. He lay back and stared at the sky through the gauzy green fabric.

"It's like the grass," he murmured. "But thinner . . . slippery . . ."

He closed his eyes, and in three seconds he was fast asleep.

He woke up a long time later. Kit was sitting across from him. He didn't know how long she had been there, watching him sleep. In her hand there was a miracle, a large orange that glowed with thunder. She tossed it up and caught it, then threw it to him.

Devin stared at it with disbelief. "Where did you get this?"

"Stole it. You've been asleep for hours."

Devin peeled the orange and divided it in half.

"Don't bother," Kit said. "I've had one already." She got to her feet and started emptying her pockets, bringing out handfuls of things, fragments of glass, screws, an assortment of bottle tops. While Devin ate, she sorted the items, examining each in turn, making little piles. When she was done, she put each pile into a different container.

"You've got a lot of stuff," Devin said.

Kit stared hard at him and shrugged.

"I collect." She reached into another pocket and pulled out a last item. "This one's a true rary," she said. "Never seen one of these before." In her palm was a tiny shell, delicately whorled. "You ever seen the ocean?"

He shook his head. "I had a book with a picture of it. It looks big."

"All that water . . . ," Kit said.

"My granddad told me you can't drink it, though. It's too salty."

"I wouldn't care about some stupid salt," she said. "I'd stick my head in and I wouldn't stop drinking until I died."

Devin got up and went to the edge of the roof to take in the view again. "Those trees," he said. "Over by the hills. I came through those when I first got here."

"You mean The Meadows?"

"Is that what they're called? The grass there, it's very green. I think they water it."

Kit stared at him, her eyes narrowed with suspicion. "Do you really not know anything or are you just pretending?"

Devin didn't know what to say

"The Meadows is where the rich live," Kit explained.

"Where do they get the water?"

"They own the water, idiot! How do you think they got rich in the first place?"

Devin thought of the sky dark with rain and the way the stream at the farm ran too fast to hold. "You can't own water," he protested.

Kit rolled her eyes. "Well, they do. They own it. They own control of it. Along with just about everything else."

"But how? How did they get everything?"

She shrugged. "I don't know. I guess they just grabbed it. And everyone else needs what the rich have, so they just go on getting richer. It's the way it is. The rich have a lot, most other people have a little, and then there's us. We don't have anything at all.

"Lots of kids in our group," she added.

"But don't they have homes?"

"Used to. Some of them had good homes before their parents died or weren't able to feed them anymore. Lots are runaways."

"What about you?" Devin asked. "Are you a runaway?"

Kit shrugged again. "My parents ran away from *me*. I came back one day and they'd left. Best day of my life."

"My granddad used to live here when he was young," Devin began. "He said it was different then. It changed when it started to get hot. People stopped looking out for each other and lots of things that used to be organized just turned into a big mess."

"Yeah?" Kit said without much interest. "Well, it's like this now. And it's not going to change. Some of the kids talk about getting out, how they heard about a kid who got adopted by rich people and went to live in luxury forever. Or that there's a home somewhere where they feed you and you can play all day and have everything you want. But it's just fairy tales." Kit's mouth set in a fierce line.

"Fact is," she said, "we're on our own."

✦ ✦ ✦

They spent the rest of the day on the roof. Along with the oranges, Kit had found a loaf of bread—completely stale, but whole. She fetched water from an old bathtub on the roof. It had been collected during the last rainstorm, and there was very little left. "You have to boil it," she told Devin. She showed him how to soak the stale bread in the water until it grew soft and could be eaten with a spoon. When the meal was finished, they sat under the canopy and talked. Kit wanted to know about the farm.

"My granddad used to say there was nowhere else like it. He said it was a place where all you had to worry about were ordinary things. Like whether the chickens were laying or how to mend a fence," Devin said. "I didn't know what he meant."

He paused. "Then I left and came here."

Kit made a face. "And now you know exactly what he meant . . ."

"I thought I'd get help with it," Devin said. "But there doesn't seem to be anybody to ask. I don't know who to go to."

"You're right," Kit said. "You can't trust anybody in this place."

"It will be getting so overgrown, and I don't know how the animals are doing. "

Kit looked away. "Don't think about it, Devin."

"I nearly went into that place that says Police," he said. "I thought—"

"You don't want to go there! They're not good people. They're criminals, some of them. They're supposed to keep law and order, but they only do things if you pay them. Like I said, we're on our own."

"I . . . guess so . . ."

To cheer Devin up, Kit started telling him about the time she'd been inside one of the houses of the rich. Her father had landed a temporary job doing the gardening there. While he was busy, she'd wandered inside. The first thing she noticed was how cool it was. There was a pad on the wall where you placed your hand and the temperature in the room immediately adjusted to your exact comfort. Everything adjusted, she said. The lights, the pillows on the chairs; even the windows automatically shuttered when the sun came in at a certain angle. The rich never had to lift a finger. In the bedroom, the closets were full of clothes arranged by color, all perfectly pressed, and there was a box with sliding drawers full of jewelry. Kit's eyes grew wide with longing at the memory. She'd pushed her hand right into the box and run her fingers through the treasures. In the kitchen, all you had to do was reach for the fridge—not even touch it—and the door swung open, and inside, it was the size of a small room, full of food that didn't even look real because there wasn't a mark or blemish on anything.

There wasn't a single thing inside or outside that house that was ugly or untidy.

"The rich don't like looking at anything messy," Kit explained. "It's like their cars. Ever notice how the windows are always dark? My dad said they're programmed to darken automatically so the people inside don't have to see anything that might upset them."

She paused. "I could have stayed in that house forever. But I had to leave. When I came out, my dad was waiting for me with a stick."

"He beat you just for going in there?" Devin was incredulous.

"Oh, no. He would have beaten me anyway. He beat me just for being alive."

✦ ✦ ✦

The next morning, Kit said she needed to go and get more food. Devin wanted to go with her, but Kit said he would only slow her down.

"You don't know anything," she said. "And you don't even have shoes. Anyone looking at you would think you're crazy." Kit shook her head. "No, there's an art to stealing. There's rules to it. Like stealing big and stealing small. Whenever I take something I always take something else that's much less valuable. That way, if I'm caught, I can hand back the small thing and they'll think it's all I took . . . You're not ready for any of that. I bet you can't even pick a lock, can you?"

He shook his head.

Kit led him to a box containing dozens of padlocks of different sizes and showed him how to insert a wire and fiddle with it until the lock came free.

"Practice on these while I'm gone," she told him. "I'll bring back something good."

But when she came back, three hours later, her hands were empty and her face was white. There was a large red welt on her forehead and the flesh around one eye was bruised.

"What happened?" Devin cried. Kit said nothing. She walked furiously across the roof, her fists clenched and her head down.

"Are you all right?" He reached out and, before she could stop him, gently touched the bruise on her face.

"Oh," he said, in distress. "Why does it taste like honey? It shouldn't taste of something nice."

She flung away from him in sudden fury. "Are you trying to be funny? Talking crazy like that! You did it before. I thought you were just tired. Are you nuts or something?"

Devin didn't know what she meant. She was just upset, he thought. It would be best if he didn't argue.

Kit went to the mattress and sat down with her knees pulled up to her chin, the shards of disc overhead casting patterns on her face. She sat there for a long time, staring at her boxes of treasures. Devin waited until he saw her shoulders relax before speaking again.

"I'm going with you next time," he said. "I don't want you to be hit again."

She lifted her head. "It's okay."

"No, it isn't."

"We'll both have to leave for a while anyway," Kit said, getting to her feet. "Look at the sky."

In the far distance Devin saw storm clouds, watery brown with blackened edges, like something singed. The breeze had completely gone and the city was held in a breathless, dusty hush.

"I think we've got till the evening," Kit said.

"No, the rain will be here sooner than that." Devin studied the sky with a farmer's eye. "Two hours, maybe less."

Kit was already busy, folding up the canopy and stowing it away. He helped her place lids on her boxes and stack the plates and camp stove. Together they dragged the mattress to one side of the roof and covered it with an old tarp, then arranged the bathtub and other containers in a long row to catch the rain.

"There's a place I go, where lots of the kids go, when it storms." She pointed across the city. "Over there. I think it was a school once. You'll have to follow me and be sure not to get lost because you'll never find it by yourself."

"'Course I will," Devin said. "Look at the streets in front of it. They almost join up in an X shape only not exactly, so the humming crackles a little around the edges. Plus the building itself is way more red than anything else for miles around."

This time Kit came right up to him, her eyes serious, almost frightened.

"What are you talking about? It's concrete and brick like all the other buildings. Dirty gray concrete."

"But it's different from the other buildings. They're all different. That's how you remember them, right? Once you've seen something, you can always remember where it is."

She searched his face. "You're not kidding, are you?" she said slowly. "I don't think you're crazy. Maybe you're just a fool."

But they were running out of time to talk about it. The sky had darkened to a dull yellow and the storm clouds were almost overhead. As they stood there, the first drops fell, huge and warm and very wet. For a moment or two they did nothing but enjoy the feeling of wetness on their skin, their faces raised to the sky, their arms stretched out. Then, as the rain fell harder, they ran to the edge of the roof and began climbing down the scaffolding as quickly as they could.

Four

By the time they got to the bottom of the scaffolding, the rain was falling in earnest. The streets were dark and full of frantic movement. Children, some half naked, whooped and danced in the spray, their skinny limbs gleaming wet, their mouths gaping. Shopkeepers were hurrying to lock up and bar their shabby storefronts, and tubs and troughs and barrels were being dragged out to catch water. It hadn't rained in a long time, and there was no knowing when it would rain again.

Within minutes the downpour had become a single, massive sheet of water pounding the ground so hard that the earth blurred and the streets turned into streams thick with dust and debris. People gasped and fled, struggling to breathe in the deluge. Even the mangy dogs had taken cover, scrambling for higher ground as best they could.

Kit and Devin ran, slipping and sliding, half blinded, calling out to each other although nothing could be heard above the massive roar of the falling water.

The abandoned school was already full of kids when they arrived. Everyone was crowded into the old gym, sitting on the floor alone or in groups. Two older boys were bouncing a ball and running up to dunk it through an empty hoop that hung crooked on the farther wall. Kit made her way through the crowd without talking to anyone and sat down in an empty corner, her bag clutched tight to her chest and her eyes wary. Devin sat down beside her, wringing out the sleeves of his shirt and trying to catch his breath. He looked around.

He recognized a few of the kids from his wanderings through the city. One boy in particular was familiar. He was taller than the others, maybe fourteen or fifteen years old, with dark, curly hair cut very short and a long, straight nose that gave him a haughty appearance. He was leaning casually against the wall, one hand in his pocket, the other playing with a plastic object that made a scraping noise and then produced a flame. Each time Devin heard the scrape, a tiny lavender star shimmered into his view.

Devin looked away, toward a group of three or four girls who were sitting together with their heads very close and their arms around each other. Farther away two boys scuffled. Right in front of him five more boys formed a circle, squatting with their pale, bony knees toward the center, playing some game with pebbles. One by one they shook their pebbles and threw them down. They didn't look at each other or even talk. When they had thrown their pebbles they picked them up and waited until it was their turn again. In the center of the circle there was a small pile of food. A slice of bread or two, a wedge of cheese, and a small, greasy patty that looked like it had been carried in somebody's pocket for a while.

Devin nudged Kit.

"What are they doing?"

She shrugged, not interested. "It's a game. They put food in the middle and whoever wins gets all the food."

"Have you ever played?"

She shook her head. Her whole body seemed tense.

"I don't play," she muttered. "I don't play with any-one. I'm better off alone."

The rain beat against the walls of the gym and dark-ened the interior. In the dim light, the children's faces gleamed pale. A smell of boredom and unwashed bodies hung heavy in the air.

"I hate it here," Kit whispered. "I can't breathe. I wish the rain would stop."

Devin looked up suddenly. The tall boy, the one who kept making the flame, was staring straight at him.

For a second their eyes met and then the boy looked away.

"Who's that?"

"I don't know," Kit said. "He's here sometimes. Gets enough to eat, by the look of him."

There was a sudden commotion among the group playing for food. A boy with sunken eyes and a ragged coat was trying to join the game. He had an apple in his hand and was pushing it forward. The apple was tiny and wrinkled, barely enough for a single bite.

"Butt out, Pesk," one of the gamers said. "I've seen nuts bigger than that."

"Unless they're your nuts," somebody else said and there was a burst of laughter.

The boy's eyes were fixed on the pile of food in the center. "I can play," he said. "I got something for the middle. That means I can play."

"Ah, let him," somebody cried.

Pesk squatted down and joined the circle. His knees were the boniest of the whole group, and Devin couldn't help noticing how hollow his chest was. When the pebbles came to him, he shook them for a long time.

"Come on, Pesk!"

The pebbles fell.

"Too bad, Pesk! You lose!"

Devin looked away, not wanting to see any more.

✦ ✦ ✦

The long afternoon passed. A few more children arrived. Some played quietly or talked or broke into petty fights, but mostly they just sat while the rain beat endlessly and the dim light grew even dimmer. At last it was completely dark.

When she was sure she couldn't be seen any longer, Kit rummaged in her bag and pulled out a roll. She divided it and pressed one half into Devin's hand.

"It has raisins!" she whispered in his ear.

Someone in the middle of the gym lit an oil lantern. By its flickering light, Devin could see the shapes of kids settling down for the night, arranging themselves under thin blankets, their bodies curled up on the floor. He ate quickly and lay down himself, his cheek resting on his hand, his eyes wide.

There was a boy lying next to him, his eyes glittering with unshed tears. It was Pesk.

Devin didn't say anything. The shadows made Pesk's eyes look even more sunken, like the dark holes in a skull. They stared at each other silently.

"D'you think it's true, what they say?" Pesk whispered at last.

"About what?"

"That there's a Home where they take you in? And alls you got to do is find it?"

"I don't know," Devin said.

"I think it's true. I heard they feed you alls the time

and you never . . . you never . . ." His voice trailed off. "They got new clothes there too. And so many toys you can play for just about forever."

"Shut up, Pesk!" somebody called out. "We're trying to sleep, here."

Pesk's mouth closed instantly, but his huge eyes never left Devin's face.

"Alls you got to do is find it," he whispered very quietly, as if talking to himself. He turned over, wrapped his arms around himself, and said no more.

Devin lay awake for a long time, listening to the rain. His hand crept to the hem of his pants where his grandmother's locket lay hidden. Inside were pictures of his grandparents when they were very young, taken not long after they'd first met. His grandmother had round cheeks and a smile that seemed to light up everything.

"She wasn't the prettiest girl I ever saw," his grandfather had told Devin, "but she was the loveliest."

Devin fingered the locket in the dark. It was solid gold and heavy, an oval shape, as clean and kind as an egg. He dozed briefly and woke before dawn, and while it was still dark he slipped the locket into one of the pockets of Pesk's ragged coat.

✦ ✦ ✦

The morning brought an end to the rain. Through the grimy windows of the gym, the sky was hard and blue again. In a little while, the heat would dry the earth,

42

turning it to dust once more. Now that the rain had stopped, the gym was loud with the chatter of children waking up and getting ready to leave. Kit was already itching to get away.

"We got lucky," she said. "We could have been here for days . . ."

Out on the street, the sudden glare made them blink and squint.

"We should look for food," Devin said.

"I want to get back to the roof," Kit said. "I want to set up my stuff."

"I'll go for food. It's my turn."

She hesitated. But she was anxious to get back to her roof, to set up her home again and arrange her treasures. "Okay," she said finally, "But be careful."

"I'll be fine."

He trotted off, a map of the city clear in his head. Before, when he had roamed the city alone, the sights and sounds around him had overwhelmed him with their multitude. But he was ready for them now. As he ran along, making for a particular street with many market stalls, he found himself starting to take pleasure in the rattling, chattering kaleidoscope around him.

At the market he paused, savoring the sensations. On one side, a pyramid of lemons made a rough trilling sound, and on another, he heard the thunder of oranges and carrots arranged in piles below a dusty canopy. A man sweeping the ground with a broom sent a flock of crows wheeling through his mind. Things clicked and sang and flittered over his tongue: the buttons on a coat, an upturned basket, the faces of passersby, the feel of the sidewalk against the soles of his feet.

Devin almost forgot he was supposed to be looking for food. He walked through the market in a kind of daze. By a stall selling pieces of fabric he stopped, his eyes dazzled by all the tangled, tickling colors of the rainbow. He turned around and found himself in front of a long table heaped with loaves of bread. They had been baked not long before, and the smell was heavenly. How golden they were! Devin reached out and touched one, curling his hand against its rounded shape, feeling the thin crust and the warmth of the dough beneath.

A large hand gripped his shoulder so hard that he yelped.

"I've got you now, you little thief!" Devin was yanked backward, his cheek pressed against a greasy apron, and then shaken so hard that he almost bit his tongue.

"Right. Under. My. Nose," the baker grunted, shaking him some more. "You think I'm stupid, do you?"

"I wasn't stealing it," Devin cried when he could catch his breath. "I wasn't stealing!"

The baker's face flushed scarlet with rage. "Just admiring it, were you? Just fondling it with your grubby little hands?"

Devin was silent.

"I'm sick of you thieving brats," the man went on. "Every day it's the same. I have to have eyes in the back of my head. Tried reporting it, but what's the point? Nothing happens. The police used to do something . . ." He paused and his eyes narrowed. "Now we take matters into our own hands."

The grip on Devin's shoulder tightened. "I'm going to take you around to the back," the baker said, "and give you such a beating you'll never look at a loaf of bread again."

Five

"I WASN'T STEALING IT. I've never stolen anything!" Devin cried in desperation.

The baker swung him around violently. "I'm going to teach you. I'm going to teach you a lesson you'll never forget."

"Let him go," somebody said.

The baker whirled around, still clutching Devin. "What was that?"

"I'll pay for the bread."

It was the boy from the night before, the tall one with the flame who had stared at Devin. He held out his hand and showed two silver coins.

"He's my friend. Let him go."

For a second the baker hesitated, and then he shoved Devin away.

"You got lucky," the baker told him as he took the money. "Try it again and I'll have the skin off your back."

The boy took the loaf of bread and walked away. Devin hurried after him.

"Thanks," he said. "I wasn't stealing it, but he didn't believe me."

The boy said nothing. His eyes were very pale, a faded blue that looked as if it had been washed a thousand times.

"What's your name?"

"Roman."

"Mine's Devin."

The boy spun away suddenly and made his way through the crowds. He stopped in the doorway of a deserted storefront.

"Where are you staying?" he asked Devin.

Devin hesitated. Kit had told him not to tell anyone about the roof. "Nowhere, really," he said.

"That's what I thought," Roman said. He paused for a long time, staring into Devin's face.

"I'd like to pay you back for the bread," Devin said. "Only my money was stolen . . ."

"Never mind about that," Roman said. "I want to talk to you."

"Why?"

"I saw you in the gym last night. I watched you. You put something into that kid's pocket. Something valuable. Something you've been holding on to for a while. Why?"

Devin felt his face redden. "I don't know . . . I felt bad for him. I figured he could buy food with it."

Roman nodded. "That's what I thought. There was nothing in it for you. It was just kindness."

His words were warm, but there was something automatic in the way he spoke them that puzzled Devin.

"Some kids are born kind, but it's rare," Roman continued. "Most have to learn it. How do they learn it? By being treated with kindness themselves. I thought the moment I saw you that you must have come from a good home. Did you?"

Devin nodded. "There was me and Granddad, and when I was very little, there was Grandma too." He thought of his horse. "And animals. A horse and a cow and chickens and we were going to get a sheep . . ."

Roman nodded. "I knew it." He hesitated, staring at Devin for what seemed like a long time.

"Listen," he said quickly, as though coming to a decision. "You ever hear rumors about a children's home, a place where they feed you and keep you safe?"

"The boy—Pesk—was talking about it. But Kit says it's just a fairy story."

Roman put a hand on Devin's shoulder and leaned in close. "What I'm about to say is not a fairy story. It's the truth. Only you can't tell anyone about it. There is a home for children and it's great. They have everything. Playgrounds and a swimming pool and beds with clean white sheets and meals whenever you want and a ton of other stuff I don't have time to tell you about right now. They take in kids who have no home of their own. I know because I live there myself."

"Why are you telling me?" Devin asked.

"They can't take every kid," Roman explained. "They have to choose. And they only choose special kids." His hand tightened on Devin's shoulder. "I can take you there. Tonight. Think about it, Devin. Tonight you could be sleeping in a bed, with a full stomach, far from this filthy city, far from danger."

"I don't know," Devin said.

Roman straightened up and took his hand away. "Well, it's up to you," he said. "But don't think about it too long. I'm leaving tonight."

"Can Kit come too?"

"That girl you were with last night?" Roman frowned. "I don't think so. No. She's not . . . she's not right for the Home at all."

"Then I can't go," Devin said simply. "I'm very sorry. Thanks for asking me, though. And thanks for saving me from the baker."

"You won't change your mind?"

Devin shook his head. "Not if Kit can't come. There's no way I'm leaving her behind."

Devin clambered up to join Kit on the roof. All her stuff had been put back in place.

"You were gone for ages," she said. "Get anything?"

Devin handed her the loaf of bread.

"A whole one! And it's fresh!" her eyes narrowed. "Did you steal it, Devin? I didn't think you'd be able."

"I didn't steal it." Devin sat down on the mattress. "It's a long story. I met a boy. He was at the gym last night. His name's Roman, and he bought it. I was going to be beaten by the baker and he saved me."

"You're not making sense," Kit said, tearing a chunk of bread from the loaf and stuffing it hungrily into her mouth. "Start from the beginning."

She listened in silence until he came to the part where Roman had told him about the home.

"That's nonsense!" she burst out. "It doesn't exist."

"But he said it did. He said he lives there."

Kit screwed up her face until her freckles almost merged into one. "Devin!" she cried. "He was messing with you. Only you would have believed him. You'd believe anything."

"I said I wouldn't go," Devin told her. "He said you couldn't come, so I said no thanks. I just walked away."

"You believed him about the home but you still walked away?"

He nodded.

"Because I couldn't come?" Her face looked as shocked as if he'd just slapped her.

"Yeah. And then he came running after me and said okay, you could come too, but nobody else. And he gave me the bread. And he said we have to meet him tonight."

"This doesn't make any sense. I don't know what this boy Roman is up to, but I don't like it. We'll just eat the bread and forget about it."

"Why?"

"Devin," Kit said softly. "You lived on a farm all your life, but even you have to know that people don't buy you bread for nothing. And people don't drive you off to homes where you can live happy ever after. Not in the real world."

Devin looked at her. She was wearing a different shirt, a ragged yellow tank that showed the top of her arms. Now he could see that there were marks all over her shoulders, a dense crisscross of scars and ugly lines of raised skin where she had been beaten. The marks were faded purple, and into Devin's ears came the sound of the farm rooster crowing, faint and far away like something in a dream. Kit saw him looking and raised her chin defiantly.

"Trust me," she said. "Good things don't happen in the real world."

"They must sometimes," Devin pointed out. "Maybe just one time in a hundred or a thousand. And if there's even just a tiny chance, don't you think we should take it?"

✦ ✦ ✦

They talked about it for the rest of the day without being able to decide what to do. In the end, they came to a compromise. They would go to the meeting place and Kit would make up her mind after talking to Roman and hearing more about the home. Kit was certain it would be nothing but a trick and they would return to the roof for the night. Still, when it came time to leave, she hesitated.

"If we do go, if it's real, I don't know what I should take with me."

"They probably have everything we need right there," Devin reminded her.

"But my raries . . ." She hovered over the small shelf where she kept her most prized finds. The shell was there along with an assortment of tiny porcelain dolls' heads, three old keys, and the golden nib of an ancient pen. Kit scooped them up and put them in the bottom of her bag.

"Okay, I'm ready."

It was dusk by the time they climbed down from the roof. They hurried through the streets, making for the place where Devin had last seen Roman. He was standing just where Devin had left him, leaning against the wall, half in the shadows.

"Come on," Roman said immediately. "We have to leave right this minute."

"We're not going with you until I find out more," Kit said. "I'm not leaving without some proof that it's not just a trick."

"There's no time," Roman said. "I'll explain everything later. You have to come now."

He turned and disappeared down a side street that was illuminated only by a few dim lights from neighboring buildings and the half-spent moon above the rooftops. The shadows fell long and dark over the sidewalk. At the far end of the street there was a car. It was large and gleaming and lit from the interior. A man was sitting in the driver's seat, his body nothing but a dark silhouette.

The passenger door was wide open, waiting.

Kit gripped Devin's arm.

"This isn't right," she said, shaking her head. "I don't like it."

Devin could feel her alarm, the beginning of panic.

"Look," he said, "You're right. We don't know anything about this. But I think we have to go. We can't stay in the city. Always hungry, having to steal, getting into fights and getting hurt. How long can we survive like that?"

"Okay, listen, this is a bad idea," Kit said, talking very fast, "I should just turn around and walk away from this. But here's the thing. You told that boy you wouldn't go without me and nobody's ever done something like that for me before. Not once. Not ever. This is a bad idea, but I can tell you've set your mind on it and someone's got to watch your back. You wouldn't go without me, and now I'm not going to let you go alone."

Kit marched forward and got into the backseat of the waiting car.

Six

DEVIN HAD NEVER SEEN anything like the inside of the car. The minute he got in, he was in a different world. Everything gleamed and the air was fresh and cool. As he sat down on the tan-colored leather seats, they made a tiny sighing sound as they shifted to fit his body. The windows—completely darkened—gave no view outside.

Roman had gotten into the front seat, next to the driver. There was a glass panel between the front and back seats. The car moved off swiftly and utterly silently.

Kit sat half curled up, her eyes wide and watchful. "I'm not going to close my eyes for a second," she whispered to Devin. "If anything happens, I want to be ready."

He nodded. "Me too."

But the cool air, the comfort of the seats, and the soft

vibration of the car as it sped onward soon lulled Devin into a doze and then into a deep sleep. He dreamed of his grandfather at the kitchen table at night with the light from the lantern making a circle of gold. His grandfather had the book open and was teaching him to read. "No, that's not it," he said to Devin in his quiet, patient voice, "you're getting all muddled up aren't you?"

"I am," Devin said. "I'm really muddled up, Granddad."

Devin looked down and the whole farm was suddenly there below him as if he were flying. And it was set inside another, bigger circle of gold that glowed bright at the edges and kept the dark away.

"You have to try again, Dev," his grandfather said, turning the page. "Go back, try again, go back."

"I can't, I don't know how! I don't know!"

Someone was shaking him, calling his name. It was Kit. His eyes shot open. It was early morning; they had been driving all night. The car windows had lightened to clear glass and he could see they were far from the city, traveling on an empty road. Beside the road he saw thin lines of crops. They were soybeans, one of the few plants that could be cultivated on such dry soil, although even these were stunted and half withered.

"You slept for hours . . ."

Devin wasn't listening. He was too busy staring outside, where a row of hills made a pattern against the sky, interrupting the steady clicking of the horizon with a series of soft thuds. He looked up and noticed by the sun that they were traveling west. The road forked and they turned away, moving southwest now, past great heaps of tumbled rocks.

A tray slid out from the panel in front of them and there were two glasses of a shimmering pale yellow liquid. Kit eyed the drink. "Better leave that alone. It's all bubbly. We don't know what it is."

"But I'm so thirsty, Kit."

"Okay. But I'll try it first."

She took a wary sip and her face shivered with astonishment. "I never had a bubbly drink before."

The car turned off the main highway and began to wind along through trees and hedgerows. The road narrowed until it became a single lane. Finally it petered out completely. In front of them was a stone arch with words carved across the top:

Gabriel H. Penn Home for Childhood

In a second, the car had passed beneath the arch and entered a long and shady driveway.

Kit cast a look at Roman sitting in the front seat. "He was telling the truth," she whispered. "There really is a home. It really exists."

✦ ✦ ✦

The driveway wound around in a wide curve. To their left were bushes and tall trees; on their right, a huge meadow, surrounded by a low fence, where three or four horses were grazing. As the car came around the top of the curve, Devin and Kit saw a group of buildings built around a courtyard, with a tower at the center. Above the tower, the sky was full of dark flecks; a vast flock of birds, which darted this way and that in sudden groups and clusters.

The car pulled up alongside the buildings and entered the courtyard with the tower. The walls around them were golden stone, faded with age and covered with patches of creeping ivy. The courtyard itself was paved around the edges, and there were beds of flowers on both sides, bright, heavy, rich-looking blooms that Devin had never seen before. They must need a lot of water, he thought. He had never heard of anyone wasting water on flowers. The extravagance of it astonished him.

The car stopped and the children got out.

Instantly the air was full of the sound of the birds twittering in their hundreds. A small girl who must have been waiting in the shadows ran forward and attached herself to Roman's side. She was six or seven, round-faced and blond, with a large yellow bow pinned to the side of her head. She peeped around Roman at the newcomers.

"Have you got a match?" she asked Devin in a sweet, clear voice.

He shook his head.

"Not even one?" the girl begged, "not even a teeny tiny baby one?"

"That's enough, Megs," Roman said, patting her on the head. "Leave them alone. Go on now." She darted off obediently, her yellow bow bouncing against her curls. Roman turned back to Kit and Devin.

"I have to go. Mrs. Babbage will be along to show you to your rooms."

"I can't believe we're here," Kit said. "You were telling the truth. Who runs this place? How long do we get to stay? How many kids are here?"

But Roman didn't seem in the mood to talk. He looked down at the ground, not meeting their eyes.

"I have to go," he repeated. "Mrs. Babbage will look after you."

As if on cue, a woman came out from one of the buildings facing the courtyard and pattered over to them. She wore a cardigan that drooped almost to her knees, and her thin hair was pinned back in a bun no bigger than a walnut. Her face wore an expression of kindness.

"Right on time!" she cried, as if the children had planned their own arrival. "You poor, dear things, you must be ever so tired."

"Not really," Kit said. "What is this place? Do you run it? Can we look around?"

"There's plenty of time for all that, plenty of time. You must rest. Your rooms are ever so nice." And she led them away, across the courtyard, into another building, and up a winding stone staircase.

They found themselves in a small bedroom with whitewashed walls and a patchwork quilt on the bed.

"This will be your room," Mrs. Babbage said, turning to Devin. "There's a bathroom over there, and your pajamas are laid out. Clean clothes in the closet. You jump into bed and have a little sleep and when you wake up you'll feel ever so refreshed."

Devin and Kit could only stare, dumbfounded.

"You're next door," Mrs. Babbage continued, turning to Kit.

"You mean I get a room too?"

Mrs. Babbage made a high-pitched tapping sound at the back of her throat which Devin thought was probably a laugh.

"Of course! All our children have their own rooms."

She darted into the hall, followed by a bewildered-looking Kit. Devin was left alone.

It was very quiet. The walls were stone, and no sound from the outside, not even the twittering birds, could penetrate them. Devin stared at the quilt on the bed. The scraps of fabric formed a complicated pattern that instantly imprinted on his mind. Large, interlocking stars were connected to each other by smaller ones, the whole piece worked in a hundred different shades of red and blue. But it was the shapes in between the stars that Devin looked at. They leapt out at him, a jagged arrangement of triangles that looked just like stairs rising and falling, turning back on themselves, leading nowhere, deceiving the eye . . .

✦ ✦ ✦

It was close to noon when Devin woke up.

His clothes had vanished from the chair where he'd left them. He went to the closet and found a pair of brand new jeans and a navy shirt. Then he went to find Kit.

For a second or two he didn't recognize the girl sitting on the bed next door, staring out of the window. Her hair was clean and hung in gleaming, blood-red waves almost to her waist. Her ragged clothes were gone, and she wore a green dress with a scarlet sash that matched her hair. When she saw Devin, she ducked her head, embarrassed.

"You look . . . so different," Devin said.

"There was nothing to wear," she muttered, "except this dress."

"I slept," Devin said. "I didn't think I would."

"Me too. Then I got up and had a shower. A shower, Devin! The water just kept on coming out. And it was warm!" She paused. "What is this place? It's not like anything I've ever seen before. There's nothing like this in the city, not even The Meadows."

"We had books at the farm," Devin said. "There was one with a picture inside that looked kind of like this place. It was a school, from a long time ago."

61

Kit stroked the quilt on her bed. "It's so lovely . . ."

Through the window, Devin could see hills in the distance, and nearer, surrounded by trees, he glimpsed water, too blue to be an ordinary pond.

"I think it's the swimming pool!" Kit cried, following his gaze. "Can you imagine?"

Devin couldn't. The swimming pool took his breath away. He wondered how many gallons of water the pool held. And all of it—every single valuable drop—was there just to give pleasure.

"I keep thinking there has to be a catch, but whatever it is, I don't care," Kit said.

"What do we do now?"

"We're supposed to go the dining room for lunch," Kit said. "That Babbage woman told me. After that someone is supposed to show us around the place."

✦ ✦ ✦

A separate building, off the courtyard and half-covered in ivy, housed the dining room. From its open windows came the noise of chattering, the clatter of knives and forks, and the smell of cooked food. Kit and Devin entered and found themselves among twenty-five or thirty children seated at long tables. At one end of the room, a table was covered with piles of plates and steaming dishes. They saw meat and pies and mashed potatoes and sandwiches, fruit of all kinds, and a large cake with white frosting. In the middle of the food stood a castle made of jelly, red and wobbling slightly under its own weight.

A boy seated near the door caught sight of them and immediately got to his feet.

"New kids, right?" He was skinny, with long, dark hair that hid half his face. He spoke fast, as if his words were trying to catch up with his thoughts.

"I'm Luke. I'm going to show you around. After you've had your lunch. I wouldn't show you around before you've had your lunch. That wouldn't make any sense."

"Excuse me?" Kit said.

Luke made a visible effort to check himself. "Sorry," he said. "I get a bit hyper around this time of day. Must be all the sugar, although that's never been proved, the link between sugar and hyperactivity. But you can't count it out." He gave himself a little shake and rapidly opened his eyes and squeezed them shut several times.

Kit stared at him uncertainly.

"Am I doing it?"

"What?"

"The thing with my eyes."

"Uh-huh."

Luke nodded. "Can't always tell. Best to know."

After Kit and Devin had heaped their plates with food, they sat down at one of the tables next to Luke and another boy.

"This is Malloy," Luke told them. "He's a pain in the neck."

"Hi, new people!" Malloy said. "Guess how many boiled eggs I can get into my mouth at the same time?" His face was perfectly round except for his ears, which stuck out on either side like the handles on a jug. "Three!" he announced.

"Triggered my gag reflex," he added. "I barfed all over the floor."

"Malloy likes to share," Luke said.

But Kit and Devin were too busy eating to pay attention. For several minutes, all they could think about was the food disappearing into their mouths. Luke and Malloy watched them in fascination.

"You can always tell the new ones," Luke commented.

"Like you'd know anything about feeling hungry, rich kid."

"Ever noticed how 'Malloy' rhymes with 'annoy'?" Luke said, his eyes twitching.

"Ever noticed how 'Luke' rhymes with 'puke'?"

Devin ate furiously, not really listening to the other boys. It was only when his hunger was completely satisfied that he was able to lift his head and look around him.

The cafeteria was filled with kids of all different

skin, hair, and eye color, all different ages from little ones to teenagers. But they were alike in the way they were dressed, the boys in neat jeans, the girls in the same sort of party dresses that Kit was wearing. Devin was reminded again of the pictures in his book, the ones that showed kids from a long time ago.

Most of the children seemed quiet and orderly, but three or four were making no effort to behave themselves. They had taken over the huge jelly castle and were busy demolishing it, attacking it with spoons, cramming it into their mouths, flicking pieces at each other and laughing wildly. As he watched, one small girl stuck her entire hand into the wet, wobbly mass, shrieking with excitement.

Devin glanced around to see if anyone else had noticed. But nobody was even looking. He looked in the other direction and saw Roman sitting next to the little girl, Megs. Devin wanted to catch Roman's attention, but the older boy's head was down. He was staring at his plate as if he didn't want—or didn't expect—anyone to speak to him. As Devin watched, Megs tugged at his arm, her face tilted toward him, smiling. Roman patted her gently, pushed his plate away, and stood up.

"Hey, Roman!" Devin said as he passed by.

Roman carried on as if he hadn't heard.

"What's up with him?" Kit asked Luke through a mouthful of spaghetti.

Luke shrugged. "Knows you don't like him."

"Why wouldn't we like him?" Devin asked, astonished.

"He's not exactly popular around here," Luke said, making a face. "Let's just leave it at that."

✦ ✦ ✦

Lunch was almost over and most of the children had left.

"I've got to show you around now," Luke told Kit and Devin. "You coming, Malloy?"

Malloy shook his head. His cheerful expression had vanished. "I just got the message from Karen."

Luke's face fell. "That's too bad . . . I'm sorry, Malloy. But maybe it's not for that. Maybe it's for something else."

"Unlikely," Malloy said, staring down at his hands.

Luke nodded. "Yeah. But you'll be all right. You haven't done it too many times."

"Will you keep an eye on Fulsome for me, Luke?"

"'Course I will . . ."

"I thought he was looking kind of pale this morning, not his usual self . . ."

Luke drew a deep breath. "Okay," he said, turning quickly to Kit and Devin. "I guess it's just us on the magical mystery tour."

"What was all that about?" Devin whispered to Kit as Luke led them out.

She shrugged, not interested. "Who knows?"

Devin stared back at Malloy. He was still sitting at the table, his shoulders hunched.

But Kit was hurrying Devin along. "Come on! I can't wait to see around this place!"

They stepped into the courtyard and suddenly he could hear the noise of the birds again. The sound was a collection of sharp threads, gray in the center but lightening to a dull violet at the edges, a mass of clotted knots that spread across the sky like . . .

"Hey, you okay?" Luke asked as Devin stared upward, dizzy and transfixed.

. . . like a net. A huge net, he thought. And they were all trapped underneath it.

Seven

THE COURTYARD AND THE tower were in the center of the Home. Around them, pathways led in all directions toward a variety of attractions. Kit and Devin followed Luke around the back of the dining room and saw a playground with swings and a slide. A little way off, a fountain in the shape of an elephant blew bubbles out of its trunk. The bubbles drifted away toward a circular track with wooden cars arranged in a row.

"Go-carts," Luke said.

Around the corner, Devin saw a huge, brightly colored shape, soft around the edges and curiously pudgy, with fat, leaning towers and a large inner area, the size of twenty beds.

"Bouncy castle," Luke said, as if reading from a list. "There's also tennis and basketball courts farther down, next to the large meadow. On the other side of the meadow there's a climbing wall and tree houses with zip lines."

"What are zip lines?" Devin wanted to know.

"Devin doesn't know what any of this stuff is," Kit said. "I know about it. I mean, I've heard about it, but he just knows stuff about farms." Her eyes were shining.

She was right, Devin thought. He had never owned toys. The farm had been his playground. The barn had been his castle, Glancer had been his steed, and a piece of whittled wood had been his sword.

They continued to walk. Although it was hot, there was shade under the trees, and a gentle breeze followed them as if, like all the other things in the Home, it had been expressly provided for their comfort and ease.

"Here's something you can relate to, Devin," Luke said.

They had stopped by a small farmyard. Devin could tell at once that it was just for show, not a working farm, but he couldn't help admiring the large pigsty and the pair of goats in the enclosure beyond. He sniffed deeply, inhaling the familiar scent of hay and manure. The breeze ruffled the grasses in the meadow, and he smiled to himself, wondering how such a soft, whispery noise could be colored so very red . . .

"Look at that!" Kit cried. Devin turned and saw horses. Not living ones, but brightly painted wooden creatures that rose and fell, galloping fixed and stately around a glittering platform roofed with gold.

"I want a ride on that!" Kit declared.

"If you want a ride, you can ride a car too," Luke said. "They're copies of old ones—real low-tech classics, except they're sized for kids. There's about ten of them in the garage.

"They can get up to twenty-five miles per hour, sometimes thirty," he added without excitement.

A little later, he led them past a group of kennels. Kit stopped, transfixed.

"Are those . . . puppies?" she asked. "Can we play with them?" She ran over to their enclosure and fell to her knees, her hands groping among the tumbling creatures.

"You can probably have one if you want," Luke said, uninterested.

Devin was puzzled. He knew that Luke had been at the Home for a while, but surely not long enough to get bored with everything in the place. Kit picked up one of the puppies, a mottled scrap of brown and white patches, all tongue and wagging tail. She pressed her face against it.

"I'm going to call him Frisker!"

"Whatever," Luke said.

✦ ✦ ✦

As they walked, Devin observed several adults, dressed in dark green. Some were tending to the flower beds; others passed by pushing carts or carrying supplies of one sort or another. They were staff members, he thought. He remembered the way his clothes had been silently removed and the huge amount of food that had appeared in the dining room. There must be dozens and dozens of staff at the Home, working behind the scenes, keeping everything orderly. He smiled hesitantly at a man walking down the path toward him with a pile of towels. But the man didn't smile back.

Devin also saw plenty of children; some seemed odd to him. One boy was walking along clutching a teddy bear to his chest although he was at least fourteen years old. A girl was crouched beside a bush, completely still, her arms wrapped around herself. That was the other odd thing about the kids. Apart from one or two, the majority of them were just sitting or standing around.

Despite all the marvels surrounding them, very few children were actually playing.

A great stillness hung over the place. From somewhere far away came the sound of music, tinkling and repetitive, the notes pink and apple green, as pale as fingerprints on a window.

Da dumdee dumdee, dum dum dum . . .

"And now . . . big drum roll, please . . . the swimming area!" Luke announced.

The swimming pool was a complicated arrangement consisting of one main pool and several smaller ones leading into it. Waterfalls cascaded down piles of rocks, and there were water toys everywhere. But only one boy was enjoying the place. He was about twelve or thirteen, broad shouldered, with a square, strong-looking face. He stood waist deep, holding a red plastic pistol in one hand. As Devin watched, he suddenly squirted himself in the face, laughed loudly, and then, seeming not to notice that he had an audience, did exactly the same thing over again.

"Who's that?" Devin asked.

"That's Ansel," Luke said, without looking.

"Why's he doing that?"

"I don't know. Don't look."

"Why not?"

Luke turned away abruptly. "Just don't, okay?"

Ansel squirted himself in the face for a third time. "Come on," Luke said roughly and hurried them away.

✦ ✦ ✦

A girl sat under the shade of a large cedar tree. She was sucking the tips of her long hair and staring blankly at the ground.

"Hi, Missie," Luke said.

Missie frowned. "Hi, yourself, rich kid. How come you get to show the new kids around? It's not fair."

Luke's eyes twitched rapidly. "You want to do it?"

"No. I'm just saying, Genius."

"Don't pay any attention to her," Luke told the others. "Missie's always crabby."

"I'm not crabby," Missie argued, tossing her saliva-wet hair. "It's everyone else that's so stupid and cheerful."

Luke rolled his eyes. "Missie's the sort of person who could be driving a car down a one-way street and if she saw twenty other cars all going the opposite way, she'd think they were the ones going in the wrong direction."

"Of course I would," Missie retorted. "If they were."

"Why'd she call you 'rich kid'?" Kit asked, after they had walked on a little way. "Malloy called you that too."

Luke stopped abruptly. "Okay," he said. "Let's get it over with. I come from The Meadows. My parents were billionaires."

Kit's eyes widened. "What happened?"

"The money wasn't theirs. They stole it. The plan was sheer genius. They got millions and millions from rich people who were hoping to get even richer. Greed makes idiots out of people, that's what my dad always said."

He looked down at the ground, scuffling the dirt with his shoe. "The trouble is, they got caught. The judge gave them ten sentences of fifty years each. That's a total of five hundred years in jail for each of them."

"But won't they be . . . dead before that's done?" Devin asked, bewildered.

Luke rolled his eyes. "'Course they will. The judge was making an example of them. If you steal money from the rich, nothing can save you. Don't you know anything?"

Kit shook her head. "He doesn't. It's not his fault."

"So what happened to you?" Devin asked Luke.

"I ran away, spent some time on the street. I was trying to figure out a way to bust Mom and Pop out of jail. Might have done it too, only I met Roman."

"You met him like we did?"

"Oh yes," Luke's voice went low. "We all met Roman."

There was a confused silence. Devin reached out instinctively and touched Luke's arm. It was tense, tight as a stretched rope. Devin tasted burned rubber and peppermint—a fleeting sensation, half bitter, half sharply sweet.

"What about the genius bit?" he said. "Why did Missie call you that?"

Luke made a laughing sound. "My IQ is off the charts. Apparently. Truth is, I just figured out a way to ace the test. It's all a matter of probability, and once you've factored in the psychology of the questions it's totally predictable and you can calculate to within a percentage point what the correct answer is. Doesn't make me a genius."

Kit stared at him. "You found a way to cheat the IQ test?"

"Not cheat. Decode. Slight difference, although it amounts to the same thing."

◆ ◆ ◆

It was late afternoon. Shadows striped the green lawns and collected in pools under the trees.

Kit stopped at a narrow path that wound between low trees. Their trunks were curled and knotted like clumps of writhing snakes. "Where does this go to?"

Luke hesitated. His twitching face was suddenly quite still. "We don't need to go down there," he said quickly. "I have to take you to the Recreation Hall." And he nudged them away, down another path.

They entered a gym with a high roof. A bunch of ropes with harnesses attached hung from the ceiling. They were there so kids could swoop from one end of the gym to the other, although none of the five or six kids in the gym was doing that. They simply stood around aimlessly. Luke hurried Kit and Devin on to farther rooms, all stuffed with toys. There were dress-up chests bursting with costumes, a small mountain of musical instruments, thousands of tiny plastic blocks in all colors of the rainbow spilling out of tubs, and stuffed animals that looked like mice dressed in clothes. One room contained three trampolines; another had something Luke called paintball and a gigantic doll house, five stories high, fully furnished down to the last tiny detail.

"Oh!" Kit cried, running forward. "It has everything."

"We don't have time to stop," Luke said. "It's getting late."

As they turned to leave, Devin halted suddenly. He had the strangest sensation of being watched. He looked around—the room was empty. There was a window set high in the far wall. It didn't face the outside and he could see nothing through it, but he had the briefest impression of a shadow behind the glass. The shadow moved and was gone.

Devin hurried after the others, who were now back in the gym. He noticed that there was a walkway around the upper portion of the gym, level with the tops of the ropes. The feeling of being watched grew to a certainty. There were people up there. Not children but adults, five or six of them, keeping so still you might not know they were there unless you were looking.

"Who are they?" he asked Luke. "What are they doing?"

The reason they were all so still, he now realized, was because they were all extremely old, older than he imagined it was possible to be. They looked like scraps held together by cobwebs and spit. Only their eyes, glittering slightly, showed that there was life inside their brittle husks. One or two stood leaning on sticks. The rest were sitting in wheeled chairs, their shrunken faces surrounded by pillows. On each face was a look of utter concentration.

Devin suddenly noticed another thing. Just a few moments ago, when they'd passed through the gym, none of the children there were moving very much. But now they appeared in a fever of animation. They were running to climb up the ropes; a few had already managed to get into the harnesses and they were swooping to and fro, screaming and whooping. The eyes of the old people passed slowly, very slowly, from one child to another.

"Who are they?" Devin repeated.

"They're the Visitors," Luke said.

Frisker wriggled wildly, jumped out of Kit's arms and scampered through the doorway. Kit immediately ran after him.

"Visitors?" Devin repeated.

Just then, Malloy came into the gym. He was holding a huge ice-cream cone in each hand. As he trotted along, he gave a slobbering lick first to one cone and then the other, his head turning rapidly from side to side. His tongue hung out, and there was ice cream all over his chin and down his shirt. His eyes were bright, almost feverish.

"Hi, Malloy," Devin said uncertainly. Luke immediately shoved him in the ribs.

"Don't look at him!"

"Why not?"

Luke gave him another shove, even harder than before.

"Because we don't. We don't look. It's the Rule."

"I don't understand," Devin said helplessly. "What's going on?"

Luke's whole face convulsed in a massive twitch. "Look, Devin, I haven't been straight with you. There's stuff I haven't told you. But I've stopped trying to explain things to new kids because they just don't believe me. They usually have to find out for themselves. You'll know more when you go to see her."

"Mrs. Babbage? Does she run the Home?"

"Not Mrs. Babbage. The Administrator. She lives in the tower. Remember the sign when you came in? The Gabriel H. Penn Home for Childhood? Well, she's Penn's daughter, and she never lets you forget it." He drew a deep breath. "Listen, Devin. This isn't a good place. They do stuff to kids here . . . bad stuff. I hate to have to tell you that. I don't even like to talk about it."

"So why don't you just leave?"

"That's the thing," Luke said heavily. "We can't."

Eight

DEVIN FOUND KIT IN her room after supper.

"I don't like it here," he said. "Luke told me nobody can leave, but I think we should try."

Kit was arranging her bed for the night, folding down the quilt carefully and plumping the pillows. She didn't look at him.

"You were the one who wanted to come. You said we should give it a chance."

Devin told her about Malloy and the ice cream and what Luke had said to him while she had been chasing Frisker.

"You know what I think?" Kit said, sounding angry. "I think Luke is crazy. I mean, just look at him, the way he twitches all the time. Why should we believe what he says? I didn't think this place existed, Devin, but it does. And it's amazing."

She fell to her knees and pulled a box from under the bed.

"I wasn't going to show you this, but look." She took a tiny golden jug from the box. "I took it from the doll-house," she said. "Isn't it the rarest of all raries?" She rummaged further in the box.

"Remember my rule? Steal small and steal big?" Inside the box lay the rest of the dollhouse dinner service, a glittering trove of plates and crystal glasses, each no bigger than a fingernail.

"Have you ever seen anything so beautiful?"

The note of longing in her voice was the same as when she had told him about the house in The Meadows.

"Kit, I just know there's something going on here," Devin said helplessly. "Something bad for us."

She looked at him steadily, her eyes fierce amid the starry speckles of her face.

"Okay," she said. "Let's say you're right and there's something bad here. My question is, how bad could it be? Because I can take bad, Devin. I've taken it all my life. I'm kind of an expert at it. But today I got fed and I got this dollhouse stuff and best of all, I got Frisker. So what I'm thinking is, if this place really is bad like Luke says and I gotta start taking it again, better here than in the city or anywhere else."

She looked sad for a moment and very lost. Then she brightened.

"Let's talk about Frisker," she said. "I'm going to start teaching him tricks tomorrow. Like sitting and fetching. You lived on a farm, Devin. How do you get dogs to do stuff like that?"

"I never had a dog," he said. "But I have a horse. I've had her forever. She's so smart and good. I taught her loads of things. I even taught her how to dance! Some evenings, after chores, Granddad would play his guitar and I'd put on shows for him."

"What did he play?"

"Mostly green stuff," Devin said, "sometimes blue . . ."

Kit made a face. "You're crazy," she said. "You know that, don't you?"

✦ ✦ ✦

It was very late, and the only sounds were the sighing of the moon and the scratch of ivy against the window of Devin's bedroom. He lay wide-eyed, watching the shadows on the ceiling.

After a while, he got out of bed and went to open the window.

He stood for a long time, inhaling the night air. The grounds of the Home were spread beneath him, the trees pooled in darkness, moonlight glittering on the roof of the carousel. He was too far away to see the wooden horses themselves and wondered if they were still turning around and around with nothing but shadows to ride them. Over to his left loomed the Administrator's tower, paler than the other buildings, almost luminous in the moonlight.

Devin's thoughts kept returning to Malloy. How strange he had looked, greedily devouring the ice cream. Luke had told him not to look, but Devin knew Luke had seen Malloy too and had shuddered.

And yet Malloy had been fine at lunchtime. Devin had liked him then, even hoped they'd be friends.

Devin returned to bed with an uneasy mind, and it was a long time before he fell asleep.

✦ ✦ ✦

It was almost noon when he woke up. Someone was knocking at his door.

A girl appeared.

"I'm the messenger," she said. She paused, waiting for him to do or say something. She had long brown hair in a center part and fingernails bitten down so far there was hardly any nail left at all. "Oh, yeah, sorry," she said. "I forgot you're new. Sorry. I'm Karen. I'm the one they always ask to give the message."

"Who always asks?"

"Mrs. Babbage or the Administrator. I don't know why they ask me. I don't want to do it."

"What's the message?"

"Oh sorry, forgot to explain that too. The message is

always the same. You have to go see the Administrator. Normally I just turn up and say 'I'm the messenger' and everyone knows what I mean."

"So I have to go to the tower?"

She nodded. "Sorry . . ."

Devin pulled on his jeans and went outside. The birds were still there, swooping to and fro around the tower. He paused at the door, not knowing whether to knock or not. He pushed it gently and it opened.

He'd been expecting to find himself in a large area, with a staircase, perhaps. Instead he was standing in a narrow corridor, more like the hallway of an ordinary house. On one side was a coat rack, on another an umbrella stand and a place for boots. The walls were painted a dull plum color, and a faded rug in the same shade ran all the way from the entrance to a wooden door at the far end of the hall.

Devin went down the corridor and through the wooden door into an even smaller room, barely bigger than a closet. It was perfectly square, without windows or furniture or decoration of any kind.

The door closed behind him.

Next second, the floor shifted beneath his feet and the whole room seemed to tremble. Devin cried out in alarm and reached to steady himself. A band of light appeared. It ran all the way around the room and as he stared, it moved down toward the floor and disappeared. There was a long, low hissing sound, and then the wooden door opened again.

Devin was shocked to see that he was now at the very top of the tower, standing in an enormous circular room. Comfortable armchairs surrounded a fireplace. Pictures hung on the curved walls: scenes of mountains and cows, and a lady in a bonnet sitting in a field. There were little tables crowded with knickknacks, and a beautiful old rug covered the floor. Half the wall on the farther side of the room was devoted to books, all bound in the same dark leather and all exactly the same size. At one side of the room was a gleaming wooden desk, empty except for a big bowl of blue marbles.

A woman sat perched on the front of the desk, staring intently at a piece of paper.

She was dressed in an immaculate white shirt and navy skirt without a single crease or sign of wear. A small key on a silver chain hung around her neck. Her dark hair was all one shape without a strand out of place, and it was very shiny. Her skin was shiny too, pale and polished and perfectly smooth. She looked, Devin thought, as if she were waterproof, as if nothing—not sweat or dirt or tears—could stick to her even for a second.

She raised her head at last and looked at Devin. There was no expression at all on her face.

"Well," she said. "So Roman has redeemed himself."

Devin didn't know what to say. She spoke extremely

clearly, her *s*'s particularly sharp, sizzling in the air above her head.

"Sit down."

He looked around and chose a high-backed chair next to a metal stand with a blanket draped over the top of it.

"You look fairly healthy," she commented. "Some of Roman's finds arrive in very poor shape indeed. But you're too thin. You're not eating enough."

"I am . . . it's just that I didn't have much before, when I was walking and then when I was in the—"

"Yes," she said, cutting him off. "You must eat more. Our food is excellent. Nothing synthetic or processed. We did a lot of research before we got it just right."

"Please . . ." Devin faltered. He looked down. He was squeezing his hands together so tightly it almost hurt. "Please can you explain what I . . . this place . . . ?" His voice trailed off.

"Remarkable," the Administrator said, ignoring his words. She was studying the piece of paper again. Devin suddenly heard a noise; a scraping, shuffling sound coming from somewhere very close by. He half turned.

"Bye-bye," someone said in a low, dusty, unhappy voice.

Devin looked around the room, startled. He could see no one apart from the Administrator.

"Bye-bye," the voice said again, even more wretchedly than before.

The Administrator strode forward and whisked the blanket off the metal stand next to Devin's chair.

"Be quiet, Darwin!"

A bird huddled on the floor of a cage. It was pale gray all over except for its tail, which was red, and a flash of white around its eye. But its feathers were dull, and there were large bare patches, as if the bird had been pulling them out. It shuffled toward Devin and gave him a sorrowful look.

"This is an African grey parrot," the Administrator stated. "It is the most intelligent of all the parrots and capable of learning hundreds of words and mimicking almost any sound. It can be taught to count and even to hold simple conversations." She gave Darwin a long, blank stare. "Unfortunately," she said, "Darwin fulfills none of these expectations. He refuses to learn anything. He has mastered merely one word."

The parrot ducked his head as though ashamed. "Bye-bye, bye-bye."

The Administrator replaced the blanket over the cage. "He deserves to be kept in the dark," she said. "Perhaps it will encourage him to try a little harder."

"But why don't you just let him go?" Devin asked, in distress. "If he's such a disappointment . . ."

"Because he is a failure," the Administrator said very sharply. "And I don't like failure, Devin. He serves as an example of the consequences of disappointing me."

She turned back abruptly to the paper she'd been studying. "You were brought up on a farm."

He nodded. It seemed the Administrator didn't ask questions. She just made statements. Perhaps this was because she already knew the answers, Devin thought. Or perhaps she was simply not very interested.

"Remarkable," she repeated. "It appears you have extremely unusual sense perception. Blending of just two senses is rare, but in your case all five appear to overlap to some degree. This level of synesthesia occurs in only one out of ten million individuals."

Devin hadn't eaten breakfast and he was starting to feel faint.

"What's syn . . . synesthesia?"

The Administrator dipped her fingers into the bowl of marbles on the desk and stirred them with a noise like teeth chattering on a cold night.

"The way I look, for example," she said. "It causes you to hear a sound."

"Tight and high," Devin said automatically. "Like something thin stretched out. But how do you know all this about me?"

She stared at him for a second. Her eyes were the only thing about her face that didn't shine. They were flat black, and they reflected nothing.

"Your brain was scanned," she said casually. "In the elevator coming up here."

"I saw a light. But I didn't know what it was."

"Of course not. The Home is designed to look old-fashioned. The furniture, the decor. The same goes for the entertainment. The pony rides, the carousel, the tree houses, the food. No detail has been overlooked for our clients. It's exactly what they remember." She lifted her chin proudly. "My father planned it that way."

"Is your father here?"

She glanced away. "No. My father is a genius," she announced. "He lives alone and rarely ventures out. His time cannot be wasted on ordinary things. Idle chit-chat, the keeping of dates, the dull demands of friends and family—one cannot expect them of a genius. He is above such things, and rightly so."

Devin was feeling fainter than ever. The curved wall of the room seemed to ripple slightly.

"You said . . . clients," he said. "Who are they?"

She frowned very slightly. "Visitors" she said. "I meant the Visitors."

"The old people? I saw some yesterday in the gym."

The Administrator smiled to herself.

The air prickled and shimmered before Devin's eyes. He leaned forward, his head down, his breath coming quick and shallow. "Could I just have a glass of water?" he whispered.

She waved her arm. "Yes, all right, go. Get what you need. But remember that you have to eat more. I need you to be healthy, Devin. You're the most unusual child I have ever come across. I'm saving you for something special."

✦ ✦ ✦

The elevator whisked Devin down with a long hiss like the sound of breath being expelled. In the hallway below, he half ran toward the front door, desperate for air. It was early afternoon and very hot. He stood still for a moment or two, leaning against the wall of the tower, trying to catch his breath.

He didn't know what she'd meant by those last words. Or by anything else she'd said. None of it made sense.

As he stood there, he noticed something by his foot, a tiny scrap, gray and curled. He peered closer and saw it was the body of a baby bird. There was another one not far away and then a third, lying close to the wall, in the shadow of the stone. He looked up. The birds must be nesting in the cracks and crevices of the tower. But there was not enough space there for all the hatchlings. They must jostle and shove in a frantic fight for life, he thought.

The birds were not singing at all. They were shrieking.

Devin turned blindly and ran.

Nine

DEVIN RAN ACROSS THE courtyard, through an arch-way, and down a path. He ran fast, thinking only of finding Kit, his breath fighting his throat. A boy was kicking a ball around on the grass, passing it skillfully from foot to foot, flicking it up to bounce against his knee and then his head. Devin recognized him from the day before; Ansel, the boy in the pool with the red water gun.

When he saw Devin coming, he caught the ball neatly and jogged over to the edge of the field. He stopped and gave a friendly smile.

"I'm Ansel," he said, tucking the ball under his arm. "You're new, right?"

Devin nodded, still panting.

"You like soccer?"

"I never played before."

Ansel looked amazed. "For real? I was hoping for some shooting practice."

"You're really good," Devin told him.

Ansel's face lit up with shy pride. "Thanks," he said. "It's the only thing I am good at. I was useless at school. But my dad taught me how to play. In the evenings, you know? Just him and me . . ." He smiled, a little sadly. "If you think I'm good, you should have seen my dad. He could've played in front of the world."

"In front of the world?"

Ansel nodded. "They used to, you know. Can you imagine?"

"Where's your dad now?"

"He got sick," Ansel said. "He didn't have enough money for the medicine . . ." His voice fell away.

"I'm sorry," Devin said. "Really sorry."

"Thanks."

They stood in silence.

"Have you seen Kit?" Devin finally asked. "She's new too."

"I don't know. What does she look like?"

"You saw her yesterday," Devin said. "At the pool . . ."

A spasm crossed Ansel's face. He shook his head.

"But you did!" Devin insisted. "You looked right at us. You were standing in the water and you were—"

"I don't remember!" Ansel burst out. He had flushed

a deep red and his hands were clenched into fists. He suddenly looked almost overwhelmed with rage.

"You're not supposed to look!" he shouted. "You're not supposed to tell!"

"I'm—I'm sorry," Devin stammered. "I didn't mean—"

"I just want some shooting practice, that's all!" Ansel continued furiously. "I just want to play soccer!" He gave the ball a kick so powerful that it flew into the air and smacked against the goalpost with a noise like a gunshot.

"I'm sorry," Devin repeated. He turned and ran back to the courtyard.

Kit wasn't in her room. He stood for a second or two, sick with disappointment. Her bed had been slept in but not made up. Half a dozen dresses lay strewn over it. Devin knelt and looked underneath the bed. The box containing her collection of dollhouse raries was still there. That meant she was here too—somewhere. He got to his feet and went to the window. Lunch must be over by now, but maybe she was still in the dining room.

❖ ❖ ❖

Kit wasn't in the dining hall or the pool or the gym. Devin hurried along, searching everywhere, his body drenched with sweat. Under the shade of a tree he spotted a small, familiar shape and rushed forward.

"Frisker!"

The puppy raised his head eagerly, already knowing

his name. His tiny stump of a tail wagged enthusiastically. Devin scooped him up in his arms.

"Where's Kit?" he whispered, pressing his face against the puppy's warm side. "Why did she leave you here?"

He walked on, Frisker trotting by his side. The sun dipped toward late afternoon. At last he found her in a little meadow, sitting by herself in the long grass. She was half-turned away from him, her long red hair falling in a gleaming sheet over the side of her face.

"Kit!"

Frisker whimpered, hesitating. Devin ran forward. "I've been looking for you everywhere!"

She held a small mirror in one hand and was staring at herself, lost in concentration.

"Kit?"

She looked up at last, smiling, seeming bewildered. It was her; he knew every freckle on her face. But her eyes were wrong. It wasn't the color or the shape. He couldn't find words for what it was, yet somehow it changed the look of her more than any bruise or burn. He took a horrified step backwards.

"Is that your doggy?" she asked, in a soft, dazed voice.

She bent her head without waiting for an answer. Her eyes returned to the mirror and she began running her fingers over her face, slowly, very slowly, as if uncertain of its shape.

✦ ✦ ✦

Devin had been sitting hunched up by the gates to the large meadow for a long time when Luke found him.

"Hey, buddy, you all right?"

Devin didn't answer. Luke squatted beside him and shook his head. "Stupid question. Stupid. Saw Kit, didn't you? That's why we don't look . . ."

Devin lifted his head. "What's going on here, Luke? What's happening?" His voice rose with panic. "You have to tell me!"

"All I know is they do weird things to kids." Luke said. "I don't know why they're doing it and I've been driving myself crazy trying to figure it out."

"Who's doing it?"

"Who do you think?"

Devin remembered the sound of the Administrator's fingers as they stirred the bowl of marbles.

Your brain was scanned in the elevator coming up here.

"Roman's part of it too," Luke said. "He goes into the city to find new kids and brings them back here. I hate him almost more than I hate the Administrator."

He rose to his feet. "Come on," he said. "I'll show you something."

Luke led Devin back past the soccer field, taking the path that ran by the side of the swimming area. The pool was empty of people, the water sparkling in the setting sun. It was quiet. Luke stopped. They were at the path

Devin had seen the day before, the one that ran between the low, knotted trees.

"We never go down here," Luke said, "unless we have to."

It was darker there, the way shadowed by the trees. Devin had never seen anything like them before; their branches were so interlocked that it was impossible to tell where one tree ended and another began. He followed Luke uncertainly. The path continued for a hundred yards and then opened out onto another courtyard. It was much smaller than the main one and contained a single building.

Luke stopped twenty feet away and stood looking up at it.

"This is where it happens," he said. "We call it the Place."

At first glance, the building looked like all the others at the Home. It was made of the same yellow-colored stone, and the same ivy crept over its weathered surface. But there was one difference. Only the third story had windows. Below was simply empty wall, apart from the narrow entrance. It made the place look odd, unfinished, like a face left blank where the nose and cheeks should be.

"What happens here?" Devin asked.

"It's hard to explain," Luke said. "Karen came to see you this morning, right?"

Devin nodded.

"You had to see the Administrator. That's because you're new. Normally when you get the message, you have to come here. Inside it's all modern, and it's set up like some sort of lab. There's a big chair and you have to sit in it and they give you an injection. I don't know what it is, but it's terrible. It hurts, Devin. Your whole body hurts. You're in pain and you dream and all your dreams are bad ones. Really bad ones."

Luke's whole body had become completely still, tensed up as if caught in a single massive twitch.

"Horrible dreams that you can't really describe or explain why they were so bad, even though you—" he broke off abruptly.

"I shouldn't think about them, I shouldn't think about them. But my mind gets into a loop, you know? Everything gets scrambled."

"Can't you wake yourself up?" Devin said.

"No, it feels like you can't. Everyone else can see that you're acting strangely, but you don't know what you're doing. While it lasts, there is no 'you.' You can't remember who you are." He broke off again, shaking his head in frustration.

"I can't describe it, there's no use trying."

"Is that what was happening to Malloy yesterday?"

Luke nodded. "Yeah. He was in the Dream. You saw how weird he was. Ansel was the same way when we saw him in the pool. That's why we don't look. Kids who are in the Dream act strange, and you don't want to see them; it reminds you of being that way yourself. And nobody wants to know what crazy stuff they did, so nobody tells."

"Kit?" Devin whispered.

Luke nodded. "They got her fast. I was surprised."

"How long will she . . . How long does it last?"

"Two days," Luke said. "It's never longer than two days. She'll be back to normal then."

"But why? What's it for?"

"Like I said, I don't know. I think it's some kind of experiment they're doing on us. Something to do with the cognitive sciences, certainly behavioral in some way, although I've never heard of any method that—"

Devin wasn't listening to Luke anymore. He was staring up at one of the windows at the top of the Place. The sun had dipped below the level of the roof, and with the glare gone, he could make out the details of brick and glass more clearly. He grabbed Luke's wiry arm.

"Did you see that?" he asked.

"Where?"

"I saw something, in the window. Up there, the one in the middle . . ."

Luke shaded his eyes and peered. "I don't see anything. What was it?"

"Something moved," Devin said. "I saw it for a second."

"What?"

Devin didn't answer. The truth was, he wasn't sure exactly what he'd seen. It had been small and thin, not pressed completely flat against the glass but slightly bent. Had it been a claw?

He pushed the thought away.

"Probably just a trick of the light or something." he said.

♦ ♦ ♦

It was growing dark as they made their way back to the courtyard and their rooms. Devin had many more questions, but he could see that talking about the Place and what went on there had upset Luke. His nerves seemed frayed to snapping.

A pale moon showed itself above the treetops. It shone on the horses quietly grazing, the neat pathways, and the ivy-covered walls with a peaceful, steady light. From the dining hall came the faint clatter of dishes, ordinary and comforting.

"It all looks so . . . normal," Devin said.

"Yeah," Luke agreed. "You'd never guess it was anything but a paradise. But every inch is wired, Devin. They've got sensors, devices everywhere, keeping track of us. The whole place is fake, like that wall of books in the Administrator's office. I was there once and I saw part of it slide back. There's a control panel behind it. Some alarm had gone off—it wasn't anything but a glitch, I guess. She told me to leave, but just before the elevator door closed I saw her switch the alarm off from that panel.

"The books are fake?" Devin was surprised. "All one thousand and ninety three?"

Luke looked startled. "You counted them? You must have been there a long time."

Devin shook his head. "They were right in front of me."

✦ ✦ ✦

Luke went back to his room and Devin went to eat supper. As he ate, a great weariness came over him. He longed for sleep, his mind almost overwhelmed with the events of the day. He had left the dining room and was just about to enter his dorm when he saw Roman coming across the courtyard. Megs was trotting behind him like a ghost, her dress and hair turned to gray in the moonlight.

Devin stopped, and Megs immediately ran to him. "Did you find me a match? Roman's got a lighter, but he won't let me hold it. He keeps it in his pocket."

Devin stared at Roman in silence.

"I trusted you," he said at last.

Roman's eyes were as pale as river pebbles washed by endless flow. He held Devin's gaze.

"Yeah," he said softly. "Yeah, I'm good at that."

Ten

DEVIN CAUGHT SIGHT OF Malloy next morning in the dining room. Malloy was cramming his mouth with scrambled egg, little flecks of it spraying in all directions. His eyes were closed as if he was in a kind of rapture. There was a mountain of egg on his plate, smothered with lashings of maple syrup and dollops of chocolate sauce.

He was still in the Dream, as Luke had called it. Devin looked away, feeling slightly sick.

After breakfast he wandered the grounds of the Home. The toys and entertainment no longer filled him with wonder or even enthusiasm, and he understood why there were so few children actually playing. Knowing you were part of some painful experiment made it hard to enjoy anything much. For all its novelty, a stifling air of sameness hung over the Gabriel H. Penn Home for Childhood. The same heaps of food in the dining room, the same sort of clothes worn by everyone, the same tinkling notes carried on the breeze.

Dumdee, dumdee, dum dum dum . . .

He saw Mrs. Babbage, hurrying along with a pile of bed linens in her arms. She stopped when she saw him.

"You're ever so pale, Devin dear," she said. "You need a treat! Go get yourself something from the ice-cream truck. You can hear it now."

"Is that what that music is?"

Mrs. Babbage's lips tightened into a smile.

"Yankee Doodle! It's such a popular tune, they play it over and over."

"Mrs. Babbage?" Devin said, finding hope in her friendly tone.

"What is it, dear?"

"This place . . . ," he began, his words tumbling out in distress. "The Administrator . . ."

"You'll have been to see her by now," Mrs. Babbage said. "Doesn't she do a wonderful job? She keeps it all ever so perfect, doesn't she? Oh yes, everything has to be just right.

"You'd think Mr. Penn would have come to admire it," she continued. "He built the Home, you know. The whole thing was all his idea. But he's not been back, not even once. I find that very strange, I must say."

"I'm worried," Devin said. "I'm worried about Kit."

Mrs. Babbage tilted her head to one side. "Oh, you mustn't worry. Kit is perfectly fine! I'm sure of it. She's such a pretty little thing. I'm sure she'll get adopted very, very soon."

"Adopted?"

Mrs. Babbage seemed surprised by his question. "Didn't anyone tell you?" she asked. "From time to time the children here get adopted. By lovely people, Devin. People who adore children. Wealthy people."

"Who are they?"

"Why, the Visitors of course! That's what they're here for!"

Devin remembered how the eyes of the old people had traveled from one child to another in the gym, and how the kids had suddenly perked up and started playing when the Visitors were there.

"Run along to the common room—it's next door to the dining room—and you'll see pictures of all the kids who've been adopted. Why, I don't think it will be long before you'll be joining them. And Kit too. Perhaps together! Wouldn't that be something?"

Devin nodded, a little bewildered by this news.

"Run along now and take a look," Mrs. Babbage urged him.

The common room was a large, comfortable space, full of deep sofas and shelves loaded with books and jigsaw puzzles. A girl was sitting reading in one corner, her legs carefully crossed at the ankles. A fly buzzed drowsily against the window. On one wall there was a large corkboard, almost entirely covered by photographs.

The photos were all of children and old people together. The old people didn't look particularly frail. They were the sort of elderly types whose faces still looked pretty much the same as when they were young, only more wrinkled. His grandfather had been like that, Devin thought, and tears rose in his eyes. He took a deep breath, blinked them away, and turned back to the corkboard. The children in the photos were all smiling. Some were hugging their adopted parents, while others played with kittens or held wonderful-looking toys, such as miniature cars and big, round, brightly colored hoops. One was standing on a stretch of sand in the sunshine, holding a large shell toward the camera while an older couple clapped and beamed.

Devin looked from one picture to another. After what Luke had told him the day before, he'd wondered why the children in the Home didn't rebel. Now he knew. They were hoping to be adopted, to find a family and a home.

His thoughts were interrupted by the girl sitting reading.

"You don't look special," she said abruptly, giving him a scornful glance.

"What do you mean?"

She licked her finger very delicately and turned the page of her book. "She thinks you are for some reason."

"Who? The Administrator?"

"Roman's back on her good side for finding you. That's what I heard."

Devin stared at her. She was about thirteen, with long, dark hair that hung in odd-shaped curls around her face and lay completely flat everywhere else. Her nails were red. Devin could see the scribbly lines of the marker pen she had used to paint them.

"I'm Devin," he said.

"Yes, I know," she said, rolling her eyes. "And you've made friends with Luke, haven't you? I'd be careful about that. He's nearly Spoiled, you know."

"You mean because he used to be rich?"

She rolled her eyes again. "No. Spoiled. Don't you know anything?"

He shook his head.

"It's not good to be Spoiled," the girl said with a smug look.

"I don't know what you're talking about," Devin said. "I have to go. I have to be somewhere . . ."

Back outside, Ansel was on the soccer field again, kicking his ball around, despite the heat. There was something almost robotic in the way he charged to and fro, but he came panting up to Devin the minute he caught sight of him.

"Hey, friend," he said in his straightforward way. "No hard feelings about yesterday?"

He wiped his hand on his jeans and held it out. Devin took it and they shook solemnly.

"No hard feelings," Devin agreed. "I'm sorry I upset you. I didn't understand about . . ."

"It's okay. I find it helps to exercise after I've been in the Dream. You know, run around a bit. It used to be I could take the edge off after an hour or two, but recently . . ." He broke off, his face creased with worry. "Recently it's been harder. I've been forgetting things. Not just during, but after, when I'm back to normal. An hour can go by and I don't know what happened. I just don't know. Does that ever happen to you?"

Devin shook his head.

Ansel bounced the soccer ball a couple of times, his head low.

"Did they really play in front of the whole world?" Devin asked, trying to cheer him up.

"You bet!" Ansel said, immediately brightening. "My dad said the crowd roared so loud you could hear it from twenty miles away. Imagine that. Everyone together, feeling the same thing."

"You'll have to teach me to play sometime," Devin said.

Ansel grinned. "Never played soccer!" he said. "How've you lived?"

Devin watched him jog away, moving the ball along with small, lightning movements of his feet.

✦ ✦ ✦

Devin decided to visit the small farmyard. It made him feel homesick, but it was a good sort of homesickness— if such a thing was possible. It reminded him of happiness and of belonging. He walked along, keeping his head down. The day before, he'd been frantic to find Kit, but now he didn't want to see her, wherever she was. He thought of the rapt way she had stared at herself and how in that moment she'd seemed not beautiful at all, but consumed by a kind of greed that was almost ugly.

The farmyard was all the way on the other side of the Home. Devin took the route that led behind the dormitories. He passed the ice-cream truck and the recreation hall and then paused by the entrance to the corn maze. He could hear voices, thin and inquiring. A group of Visitors was approaching, two or three men and a woman in a motorized chair that made a whining, wheezing sound as it rolled along. Devin remembered how the old people had stared at the kids in the gym, the concentration on their faces. Without hesitating, thinking only of avoiding them, he plunged into the maze.

The maze was made of corn, the stalks rising to a

height two or three feet above his head. It wasn't ripe yet—the ears were still tightly wrapped—but the leaves were tired and dry-looking, and they made a shifting, rustling sound that seemed to come from every direction, despite the stillness of the air. Devin trotted rapidly down the first dusty path, and, within seconds, the entrance was lost to view.

Inside the maze, the rustling was much louder. Grass made a red sound when the breeze passed over it, but the sound of the corn was a dull, speckled mustard that was not nearly as nice. He turned left at a fork, heading for the center, which was marked by a flag, visible above the tops of the plants. He was just about to slow down when he heard the Visitors again, the old lady's voice high-pitched, excited.

"Are we having an adventure? Oh dear, oh dear."

They must have come into the maze behind him. Perhaps it was part of the tour. Devin set off running again. The path twisted and then forked once more, seemed to double back on itself, and then continued in the wrong direction. Ordinarily he would have had no trouble at all finding his way through, but panic had seized him.

"Oh dear, oh dear, dear, dear . . ."

The voices were behind and then in front, cutting him off. He thought it must be his hearing. Old people couldn't move that fast. Devin was sure they hadn't seen him entering the maze. But still, he wanted to get away from them.

He turned around frantically and retraced his steps. The second fork again—had he turned left or right? Every turn looked exactly the same. He plunged left and then left again, feeling sure that he was on the right track until he came around a narrow corner and saw he had arrived at a dead end.

He stood very still, listening. There was no sound but the rustling of the corn. Then he heard it, the faint, ugly whine of the motorized chair. It was growing louder by the second.

Devin turned blindly and pushed his way into the hedge of corn, stepping deep into the tight, dark forest, moving as quietly as he could. He thought he could hear voices, but they were distant and soon vanished. His heart was beating hard. He put his hand on his chest to steady himself. They had gone, he thought. He was safe. They hadn't found him.

But so what if they had found him? Now that he was calmer, Devin began to feel a little silly, cowering in the dark. He couldn't imagine how he could have thought he was lost. The maze was simple; the exit was only a few turns up ahead. He was just about to push his way out of the corn and forget about the whole thing when he stopped short.

Someone was walking on the other side of the hedge.

He saw shoes. The corn stalks were too thick to see more than a vague shape of a figure. But the shoes he saw. They were men's shoes, shiny and elegant, the toes slightly tapered, the laces tied in a perfect bow. They were moving extremely slowly, coming toward him. There was a cane too. Devin saw the tip of it, a dull gold color, as it was placed by the side of the shoes.

He froze instinctively, his breath catching in his throat.

The shoes were very close now. Devin was near enough to see the tiny puff of dust as the cane came down with each slow step.

The shoes came level with his hiding place, and then they stopped. Devin slowly raised his eyes. Then the corn was moving in front of him, being parted. He saw the cane first and then the man holding it, using it to push the plants aside.

The man's face was all bones, as if the juice had been sucked clean out of it. He wore a dark suit that hung from his shoulders the way clothes hang on a scarecrow that is made of nothing but stick and straw.

"I see you," the Visitor said in a soft, playful, sing-song voice.

For a moment, Devin was too terrified to speak.

"Playing hidey-and-seek, are you?"

"I was just . . . I was just . . . ," Devin stammered.

The old man lowered his cane.

"Just having fun?" He chuckled lightly, the sound crackling in his throat. "Just playing, were you?"

Devin stared at him.

"I got left behind," the Visitor explained. "Old legs not what they used to be." His throat crackled again. "Not like yours, eh?"

Devin crept out of the corn.

The Visitor waved his cane. "Well, run along, then, don't worry about me."

Devin tried to smile, but he couldn't. The man was staring at him with a fascination that was almost disturbing. Devin turned and hurried away, not looking back even once. But he could feel the man's gaze on him watching, watching until he disappeared from view.

Eleven

MALLOY AND LUKE WERE at the farmyard when he arrived, still shaken from his experience in the maze. He could tell at once, by the easy way Malloy held himself, that he had recovered from his visit to the Place and returned to normal. But what he was doing still seemed a little crazy. He was down on his hands and knees with his face pressed up to the fence of the pigsty. Through the cracks in the fence, Devin glimpsed the snout of a piglet. Malloy, he realized, was trying to kiss it.

"Malloy! I'm Devin, remember?"

Malloy turned his head and grinned. "Meet Fulsome," he said, getting to his feet.

The piglet was only half grown but extremely fat. Its eyes were squeezed to pinpricks, and its tight pink belly almost scraped the ground. At the mention of its name it lifted its head and began to turn around and around on the spot, grunting in excitement.

"Poor impulse control," Luke commented. "Just like Malloy."

"Why's he so fat?" Devin wanted to know.

"He's not fat!" Malloy protested. "He's pleasantly chubby."

"No, he's fat," said Luke. "He's a lump of lard. Malloy feeds him scraps all the time."

"Here, Fulsome!" Malloy called. At once the pig came waddling over. "How many fingers am I holding up?" Fulsome grunted three times. "Good pig! And now?" The pig gave a single snort.

"Yes! What about now?" Malloy asked, putting both hands on top of his head. Immediately the pig, fat as he was, raised himself on two legs and began strutting around in the mud.

"Incredible!" Devin laughed.

"Malloy and that pig are soul mates," Luke said.

"I've got a thing for animals," Malloy boasted, pulling a large piece of toast from his pocket. "Watch this!" He positioned the toast in his mouth, bent down and allowed Fulsome to attach his jaw around the other end. For a few seconds, boy and pig were face-to-face, both steadily munching until Fulsome tossed his head impatiently and snatched the remaining bread away.

"Gross, right?" Malloy said.

"Sick," agreed Luke. "Get him to do something else."

"Throw that stick," said Malloy.

Luke picked it up and tossed it to the far side of Fulsome's pen. "Fetch it, Fulsome! Fetch it!"

The pig stared hard at Luke. Then he trotted over, took the stick in his mouth and returned it with a shake of his tail to Luke's feet. Luke tossed him a scrap and Fulsome gobbled it greedily.

"He's amazing," Malloy said lovingly. "Cheers me up."

"Everything cheers you up," Luke pointed out. "He's always happy," he added, speaking to Devin. "That's because unlike everyone else around here, he thinks his parents are going to come and get him."

"That's right, Professor Twitch," Malloy said. "They'll find me, all right. And if I could just get out of here, they'd find me a whole lot faster."

❖ ❖ ❖

Malloy's parents, Devin learned, were Nomads. He had no idea what this meant until Luke explained that Nomads were people who had given up on the city and on struggling to make a living and instead lived in the middle of nowhere in tepees made out of sticks. They wanted to live close to nature because they thought the only way the planet could be saved was if they wandered around admiring rocks and trying to communicate with Mother Earth. Luke sounded rather scornful when he said this. Devin glanced at Malloy, but Malloy simply nodded.

"Yup, that's pretty much it," he agreed. "It's kind of cool. Not much to eat, though . . ."

The other thing Nomads did was take long treks into the wilderness. Most of the time, they stayed in their camps, but every so often, they went off by themselves to a far-off canyon or the top of a mountain.

"It's to gain wisdom," Malloy explained solemnly. "It's really important to us."

Only adults went on the treks, so Malloy's parents had left him with the rest of the camp when the time came for them to set off. They were gone for a long time. The treks were hazardous, with dangers of all kinds, including hunger and thirst and the perils of unfamiliar terrain. When Malloy's parents still hadn't come back after two months, other people in the camp started shaking their heads, first in worry and then in sorrow. A month after that, the whole group had to break camp and move on to find food. Malloy went with them, but he slipped away the first night and returned to the ruins of the old camp. He waited alone for his parents to come back.

"I knew they just got lost," he explained. "My dad has a terrible sense of direction and my mom does everything he says cuz she thinks he's great. I figured they were out there, walking in circles, making each other laugh like they always did . . ."

Behind Malloy's back, Luke glanced at Devin and shook his head.

Malloy had waited in the camp for seven or eight days, living on tiny scraps of leftover food and searching for plants that were safe to eat. At last, hunger drove him to move on. One day he walked three miles to the south, finding nothing but dust and rocks and coyote tracks. He came down a bank of loose stones and found himself by the side of an empty road, stretching far into the distance. A single car, the sunlight glinting on its polished sides, was coming toward him. When it reached him, it stopped and the window glided down silently.

"Need a ride?" somebody said.

It was Roman.

"He was on his way back from the city," Malloy explained. "Only I didn't know that then. He asked me where I came from and who my parents were. Then he said he would take me somewhere they could keep me safe while they looked for Mom and Dad. Instead, he brought me here."

He paused. "I know they're still out there. I know it."

Luke squeezed his shoulder quickly. "Of course they are! And they'll find you, any day now. Right, Devin?"

Devin nodded.

"You'll be back in your teepee, eating gophers and getting wisdom and all that Nomad crap," Luke said. "You'll see."

"Gophers are really good," Malloy said, immediately cheering up. "Especially when they're all crispy . . . little bit of sage . . . you should try 'em." He looked from Luke to Devin. "When Mom and Dad do get here, I bet they take you away too. I won't leave without you guys."

"Good to know, my man," Luke said, a touch sadly. "Good to know."

◆ ◆ ◆

"You don't think Malloy's parents are really going to come get him, do you?" Devin asked Luke.

"If I was going to quantify the level of certainty, I'd estimate the probability would be infinitesimally low."

Devin just stared at him.

"No," Luke said. "No, I don't think they're going to come get him. I doubt they're even still alive."

They were talking in Luke's room. It was so untidy that it was a while before Devin could even locate the bed underneath all the clothes and snack wrappers. Pieces of paper lay scattered everywhere. Even the desk was a mess, with one entire edge splintered and ragged. The minute Luke sat down at it, he began automatically plucking at the wood, his fingers nervous and busy.

Devin noticed a smallish, framed photograph among the scraps of paper on the desk. It showed a smiling man in a sailor's cap and a woman with sleek blond hair by his side.

"Is that your mom and dad?"

Luke nodded. "On our yacht," he said with a curl of his lip. "The good ship *Swindler*."

"You've seen the ocean?"

"Sure," Luke said, his fingers tugging frenetically at the edge of the desk.

"Listen, don't tell Malloy what I said about his parents," he said abruptly.

Devin shook his head. "No, 'course not."

"Believing they'll come back keeps him happy, and Malloy, well, he cheers everyone up."

"I won't say anything," Devin assured him.

"The trouble is," Luke continued, "he won't stop nagging me to help him escape. He doesn't want to be adopted. He doesn't think he needs it."

"I was wondering about that," Devin said. "I don't see any fences in this place. So what's stopping us from leaving?"

Luke gave him a horrified look. "I didn't tell you?" He rubbed his forehead, very agitated. "I'm losing it, I swear. My mind's so scrambled . . . Look, whatever you do, don't try to leave."

The reason there were no fences, Luke explained, was that the Home was surrounded by twelve posts. Anyone trying to pass them would activate a laser. It wasn't strong enough to kill; it would simply disable with extreme pain. A week after Luke arrived at the Home, another new kid tried to cross. The pain was so bad she couldn't even scream; she just lay there on the ground until the staff came to pick her up.

"Malloy wants me to figure out a way to get around the posts. I've been trying, but so far, no luck."

Devin bent and picked up one of the many pieces of paper scattered on the floor. It was covered with mathematical equations, all of them tiny and set close together. They filled up the whole page, even the margins, and Devin could see that they'd been written by someone pressing down so hard on the paper that it was half curled up from the pressure.

"Does this have to do with figuring out the posts?"

Luke glanced over uneasily. "No, that's nothing. I just play with numbers, that's all. When I get stressed, you know?"

Devin's eyes swept over the room. There were hundreds of similar pages.

"It's hard to turn off," Luke said. "Sometimes I'm up all night doing it. But it's just math, you know? It's not like I'm going crazy or anything."

◆ ◆ ◆

It was particularly hot that evening—a dry, stifling heat that seemed only to intensify as darkness fell. A few children were in the pool. They stood up to their chests, not moving, trying to stay cool. Devin joined them. He had never been in such deep water. The stream at the farm had only come just above his knees, and it had felt different against his skin.

"The water's pure," his grandfather had told him. "It comes straight from the heart of the earth. You can drink it all your life and never get sick."

Devin thought of the colored pebbles at the bottom of the stream and how he had fished for them and then arranged them in lines so they would make songs, the notes trickling golden like the stream itself.

Luke and Malloy were in the pool too, as well as Missie and Karen, who seemed to be friends. The scornful girl from the common room was with them, her hair pinned up carefully on top of her head. Devin had found out from Luke that she was named Vanessa. A chunky, sandy-haired boy with a blank expression stood a little way apart, swirling the water slowly with one hand.

The only light came from two or three low torches planted nearby. The water was as dark as oil, and odd, flickering shadows traveled across the surface. The children stood in inky circles that slowly spread out to join one another and rang softly with a strange reluctance. Devin thought they sounded almost sticky.

"I'm so hot," Missie complained. "Even the water's hot. Why can't they make the water cool?" She flung her arms out, splashing.

"It's better if you keep still," Karen said.

"I know that, Smarty Pants," Missie said.

"Yeah, sorry." Karen whispered. "Sorry."

Missie splashed again.

"Stop doing that!" Vanessa cried.

"Why? You scared your hair will get wet?"

"You are so immature," Vanessa said, in a superior tone of voice.

"You okay, Malloy?" Luke asked. Malloy's mouth was turned down. Little beads of water clustered in his hair and shimmered slightly in the dim light.

"Just thinking about being in the Dream," Malloy said. "I always dream about eating. My whole body is begging to stop but my mouth won't let me. It makes me feel . . . ashamed. And what I'm eating makes it worse. It's all weird, disgusting stuff. Liver and seaweed dumplings and deep fried giblets and swan tongue sandwiches with the crusts cut off . . ."

"Coming from someone who likes to eat gophers, that's a bit much," Luke muttered.

"What's it really like, being in the Dream?" Devin asked, although a big part of him didn't want to know. The kids looked at each other and nobody answered.

"It hurts," Missie said, finally. "Sometimes more, sometimes less. Afterward I want to punch things and kick people and stamp on ants."

"Poor ants," Karen murmured, "They haven't done anything."

"They run around, don't they? They exist."

"That doesn't make any sense," Karen said feebly.

Malloy interrupted them. "Being in the Dream is weird. It's confusing, mainly. You dream that you're in a room, only you don't know where. Except, of course, you're not really there at all. Instead you're running around the Home acting weird." He paused. "That's just the start of it, though, cuz while you're dreaming that you're there in that room, you dream you fall asleep and then the really bad dreams come. The really nutso ones. They're like . . . dreams within the Dream. And they're terrible."

"I had this one dream," Luke said. "It was about animals. Or parts of animals. Their heads. I'd killed them, and cut their heads off and stuck them all over the wall. They were stuck there, but in the dream, I was stuck too. I was sitting in a chair and I couldn't move any part of my body at all. All the animals were looking down at me. Some looked like they were screaming, others just looked . . . sad. Like they knew I'd murdered them."

"My dream doesn't sound that creepy, but it was," Karen said timidly. "I dreamed I was knitting a scarf."

Missie rolled her eyes. "I wish I dreamed I was knitting."

"But it was horrible," Karen protested. "I couldn't stop. I'd been knitting the scarf for ages and ages, fifty years or a hundred, maybe. I'd started making it for a little boy but the little boy died. I don't know how I knew that, but you just know things in dreams, don't you? He'd died, but I kept on knitting the scarf for him. It was very long. I looked down and it stretched all the way to the door and I could see it curling around down the corridor. And . . . and it was wet." Karen's voice dropped very low, almost to a whisper. "It was all wet with crying."

"When I say it out loud," she continued, "it doesn't seem like much, but it's the feelings, you know? All the dreams have such terrible feelings . . ."

A deep silence fell over the children.

"That's nothing!" Malloy burst out. "I'll tell you what's really creepy."

The others all looked at him apprehensively. Devin wasn't sure he wanted to hear about another bad dream.

"People who can fart the alphabet!" Malloy spluttered. "I mean, that's just wrong."

There was a stunned silence and then a wild splashing as Missie and Karen shrieked with laughter and Luke dived on Malloy, trying to dunk his head under water. Even Vanessa smiled, although she pretended not to. Only the sandy-haired boy seemed unaffected. He stayed quite still, his face expressionless.

When the hubbub had died down, Devin asked the others about the silent boy. His name was Pavel, and he'd stopped speaking about a week earlier.

"He's really close to being Spoiled," whispered Missie.

"I heard that word before," Devin said. "What's being Spoiled?"

"Shhhh. Not so loud."

Vanessa waded across the pool and climbed out. Devin watched her pale body disappearing into the dark.

"She used that word too. 'Spoiled.'"

"Don't pay any attention to her," Luke advised. "She thinks she knows everything. She thinks she's so grown up, but she's not."

"She curls her hair," Karen informed him. "Only she forgets to do the back of it."

"But what is being Spoiled?" Devin persisted. "What's it actually mean?"

No one replied.

"Being in the Dream . . . ," Malloy began unwillingly. "It does something to you. It messes you up. After a certain number of visits, you go . . . strange."

"When kids first arrive here," Luke said, "they're normal. But little by little they start to change." He glanced around. "It's true of all of us, whether we want to admit it or not. After a while you go completely weird. Like Pavel. And Jared, the boy with the teddy bear. And Megs." He paused. "Ansel too. He's different, not in control . . ."

"What happens to you after you're Spoiled?" Devin asked.

"Everyone gets adopted," Karen said, "sooner or later. Only I hope with me it'll be sooner. I've been here for three months. Jared's been here ten months. Megs has been here for ages."

"How many visits does it take to get Spoiled?" Devin asked.

Luke's arms were wrapped around himself so tight it looked as if he might crack his chest.

"Depends on the kid. Twenty seems about . . . average."

Devin stared at him, thinking about what Vanessa had said. He wondered how many visits to the Place Luke had made. But the urge to ask questions had suddenly left him.

Twelve

THE NEXT MORNING WAS so exactly like the one before that Devin felt he had been at the Home for years rather than just three days. On his farm there had been constant activity, seasons of growth and labor, colors that sang with different voices as the months turned. And the city was full of movement too; to stay still there was to die. But here time seemed to pause. Time and the children too, all of them in limbo, waiting.

The only new activity was in the small meadow where staff members were setting up tents. Mrs. Babbage was overseeing the job.

"We're having a campout!" she told him. "We'll sing songs and roast marshmallows over the fire and sleep under the stars. It's ever so much fun. I'm sure you'll love it, Devin. The Administrator wants everyone to be involved."

"So everyone has to do it?"

"Everyone wants to," she corrected. "It's a group activity. We have group activities of all sorts. Last week we had sports day. There were all sorts of races, and the winner got a medal and so did everyone else."

"Why would you get a medal if you don't win?"

"We're all winners here, Devin."

Devin looked at her carefully. She was so kind, so warm and chirpy, despite her timid manner and droopy clothes. Devin couldn't believe she had any idea how bad it was for the kids in the Place. He thought maybe she was just dim.

He smiled politely and walked on.

✦ ✦ ✦

Devin was passing by Kit's room and saw that the door was ajar. Kit was sitting on the floor with her arms wrapped around her knees, her head down. Frisker was curled up against her ankles. Devin knew at once that she was back to normal.

"Hey, you okay?"

She looked up at him with a tear-stained face and then buried her head again.

He went over and sat down beside her, not saying anything. He could see the top of her shoulders as she leaned forward, the old scars and welts clearly visible above the neckline of her pale green dress. They sat together in silence for a while.

"Can you talk about it?" Devin said at last.

Kit sniffed and wiped her nose.

"She wanted to see me early," she said. "I had to go to the tower. You weren't up yet. When I got there, she looked angry."

"The Administrator?"

Kit nodded. "She said Roman shouldn't have brought me because . . . because I wasn't right for the Home. She knew I'd been badly treated. She said I was damaged."

Devin clenched his fists.

"I thought she was going to send me away and I'd lose Frisker and . . . and everything. But then she started talking about a shortage of something and how it couldn't be helped. I didn't understand. Not that it mattered much. I don't think she's the sort of person who cares if you understand or not."

Devin nodded.

"She said it helped that I was 'unusually attractive,' which I thought was really stupid, but I didn't argue because I wanted to stay so badly. She told me to go to this special building and I had to go right away."

"I've seen it," Devin said.

"They gave me a shot," Kit said. "Then I had this horrible feeling . . . You know how sometimes when you're just going to sleep and you think you're falling and you kind of jerk awake?"

He nodded again.

"It was like that, only it lasted for ages, that feeling of falling, and I didn't wake up. I dreamed a lot. Bad dreams mainly, really bad ones."

Kit said the dreams were strange because in the past, sometimes she had nightmares where everybody was looking at her. But in the Place, it was just the opposite; she dreamed that nobody was looking at her. It was as if she was invisible, but instead of feeling glad about this, she felt terrible, lonely and ignored and full of sadness. In the dream she came to a hall of mirrors, but even she couldn't look at herself. She crouched and covered her head, overcome by panic and shame. She kept having this same dream, over and over until she thought she might go crazy.

"I hope I never have to do it again," she said. "Because I don't know if I can take it."

"You probably will have to do it again," Devin told her. "All the kids here have done it lots of times."

Kit looked at him with anguish on her face. "But why, Devin? What's it for?"

Devin wondered what he should tell her. Everyone he'd asked had a different theory. There was Luke's idea that the whole thing was a scientific experiment. He said some of the other kids agreed with this, although a few of the younger children were convinced that magic was involved, that it was some sort of spell or enchantment and the Administrator was a witch in disguise. Karen had just shrugged her shoulders. She didn't know and she didn't like thinking about it. Thinking about it made it worse, she said. Vanessa—source of all gossip and rumor—claimed she'd heard that it was all a test.

"A test?" Kit asked when he explained this to her.

"To see if we're . . . ready for adoption," Devin said. "But I don't think that can be right. I mean, who would do that just to—"

"That's it!" Kit interrupted. "That's got to be it." She scrambled to her feet, her face suddenly eager. "It's a test to see who's ready for adoption. Or to get us ready for adoption." She picked up Frisker and buried her face in his fur. "That's it, isn't it, Frisk? And when I do get adopted, I'm taking you too."

"I don't know," Devin said. "It just doesn't sound right. I think Luke's idea makes more sense."

"I can take it if it's a test," Kit went on, ignoring him. "I can take a hundred visits to that place if it'll make me ready for adoption."

"But it's bad," Devin protested. "It makes people strange. The other kids call it being Spoiled . . ."

But Kit wasn't listening to him. She wasn't even looking at him. She was playing with Frisker as if he hadn't spoken at all. For the first time since they'd become friends on the city rooftop, Devin felt distance between them.

"There's a campout tonight," he remarked awkwardly, trying to change the subject. "We have to go. It's a group activity."

"A campout!" Kit exclaimed brightly, her voice a little too loud. "Wonderful! Great!"

✦ ✦ ✦

The campout was neither wonderful nor particularly great, despite the fact that Mrs. Babbage kept hovering around, clapping her hands and telling everyone that it was all "ever so much fun!" There was a fire and there were marshmallows on sticks and small lanterns inside every tent. But none of the children looked like they were enjoying themselves.

Devin was sitting next to Pavel, who had been sent to the Place that morning and was now in the Dream once again. He had caught a couple of moths fluttering over the dusky grass and was slowly pulling them apart, flicking the scraps of wings into the fire with a contented, almost peaceful expression on his face. Devin looked away, repulsed. Everyone else had also averted their eyes, although Devin sensed that there was something more to it than simply not liking to look at poor Pavel. He saw how the children shrank away, their bodies still, almost frozen. Devin was reminded of a rabbit he had once seen, caught in the open, under the shadow of a gliding owl. The animal hadn't tried to run or hide. It had simply stayed there, rooted to the spot with fear.

The children were like that. They didn't just dislike seeing someone in the Dream. It seemed to terrify them.

On the other side of Devin, Luke poked angrily at

the fire with a stick, the light making his eyes look dark and sunken. Kit sat in silence, her face expressionless. Only Malloy seemed to be making the most of the group activity. Having grown up as a Nomad, he was an expert at cooking over an open fire, and he was busy wrapping small packages in leaves and placing them carefully among the coals. He left them there to cook for a few minutes, then fished them out again.

He wriggled his way in between Devin and Luke and offered them each a package. They were very hot, and the boys had to pick the leaves off carefully before eating them.

"That's kind of good," Luke said, chewing. "What is it?"

"Grubs, mostly," Malloy said. "And some mashed potato to hold it together."

Luke made a terrible face and spat.

"Lots of nutrition in bugs," Malloy informed him. "Mom makes a great beetle-chip cookie. Not what you're used to, though, is it, rich kid?"

"Not exactly."

Kit had been quiet all evening, but now she seemed to come to life. "What's it like living in The Meadows?" she asked eagerly. "I bet it's lovely. Everything you want."

"I guess so," Luke said, frowning. "But when you're used to something it just feels ordinary. I spent a lot of time at school. I qualified for Hi-Speed Learning. Not many kids qualify because the program can mess with your head. But once they hook you up you can cover a whole grade in a month."

Pavel had finished with the moths and had started picking at a large scab on his knee, levering a fingernail underneath it with deep concentration.

"Hurts so good," he remarked in a small, sticky voice to nobody in particular.

He can talk when he's in the Dream, Devin thought. The realization disturbed him almost as much as what Pavel was doing, although he didn't quite know why.

Mrs. Babbage jumped to her feet and waved her arms. "Time for songs!" she announced.

"Oh, no." Luke groaned.

Devin didn't know any songs, and he wondered how Mrs. Babbage was going to persuade the kids to start singing. She didn't even try. Instead, music began to play from speakers hidden somewhere nearby and he heard a recording of children's voices.

The recording went on and on. The song was all about walking in the woods with backpacks on, and there were many verses. After it was over, another song began, and then a third. The children sat stiff with boredom. There was a movement beyond the fire, and out of the corner of his eye, Devin saw three or four Visitors, standing and nodding to the music. One was extremely fat and unable to nod because he didn't appear to have a neck. His head merely bobbed to and fro on the flabby layering of his many chins. The moment the other children caught sight of the Visitors, most of them began singing as heartily as they could.

"Hiking! Hiking! Hiking all the day!

"We have stout boots and we know the way!

"The world is full of great de-light . . ."

"Until you get a big bug bite!" Malloy sang in Devin's ear. He rolled his eyes and grinned.

The Visitors wandered away and the children stopped singing. Mrs. Babbage turned the music off abruptly.

"Tents, everyone!" she called.

Devin was sharing a tent with Malloy, Luke, and Ansel. Kit was in the tent next door with a couple of other girls. After they had all crawled inside, Malloy made an announcement. "Nobody go to sleep," he said. "I want to go look at the posts again."

Luke groaned slightly. "We've tried this before, Malloy. I can't figure out what sets off the lasers, let alone how to keep it from happening."

"We haven't tried using fire."

Luke looked thoughtful. "True."

They waited in silence, listening to the voices and rustling of children in the other tents, the footsteps of adults passing to and fro. At last all was quiet. Malloy stuck his head out of the tent cautiously. "Eagle One to Eagle Two," he said. "We have clearance."

"No one out there at all?"

"That's a negative, Eagle Two."

"Stop talking like that," Luke hissed in irritation.

"Order acknowledged. Over and out."

They emerged and made their way quietly through the camp. Kit stuck her head out of her tent and then hurried to join them. As he passed the fire, Luke picked up a stick. It was still burning slowly, the tip white with heat. They left the camp and passed by the farmyard, Devin stumbling along on the uneven ground. Where the path ended, they pushed through bushes, Malloy leading the way. He stopped about ten feet from the first post, and they stared up at it. It was made of slender steel, and a red light flickered on the very top, casting a weird, unearthly glow.

"That shows it's active," Malloy told him.

Together, Luke and Malloy had tried throwing different things past the posts, trying to see what set the lasers off. They'd thrown plates and toys, handfuls of earth, rocks and sticks. Malloy had once even flung his underpants. But nothing worked. In the end, Luke had concluded that the posts were only triggered by living things. This meant they were probably heat sensitive, and if so, it might be possible to cross them by somehow masking the natural warmth of their bodies.

"Only safe way to tell if they're heat sensitive is with this stick," he said.

"Go on, then," Malloy urged, "Throw it over!"

Luke swung his arm far back and hurled the glowing stick. For half a second they watched it, bright against the dark sky. It flew past the post and landed in a dusty patch on the far side. They waited, holding their breath.

"Nothing!" Luke said in disgust. He sat down heavily on the ground and began chewing his lip.

Malloy was still peering after the burning stick. "It's gone to join all the other stuff," he remarked. "Wonder if it'll set my underpants on fire . . ."

"I don't get it," Luke said. "If it's not triggered by heat . . . perhaps it's set off by a heartbeat."

The others sat down, disappointed. Devin leaned against the trunk of a tree and looked up. The sky was clear and the stars looked very close, as if they were hanging like decorations from the branches. He gazed at them, marking their familiar places. Kit crept up and joined him.

"What do they look like to you?" she asked him.

"Why'd you say that? They're stars."

"Tell me."

"Well, okay," Devin said uncertainly. "It's the sound first, isn't it?"

It was a keen, sharp sound like a knife running over stone, although it didn't feel as if it would cut him. It was more like a long, tingling shiver in his fingers, and then immediately afterward came the echo, and the echo sent out circles, like ripples on the surface of a still pond when a stone is thrown. The circles were gold, but only faintly, so that he felt them more in the back of his eyes and on the tip of his fingers, like something slippery that he couldn't get ahold of for more than a second.

"That's why you keep looking at stars, isn't it?" Devin said. "Because you feel you can almost hold them." He stopped, a little out of breath, feeling foolish for describing something so very obvious. Kit was staring at him with a peculiar expression on her face. Luke and Malloy stared at him too.

"What?" Devin said.

"Do you hear sounds and feel stuff when you look at everything?" Kit said at last.

"Not everything. Lots of things are sort of flat and don't make any noise at all."

"It's, like, your imagination, right?" Luke suggested. "You see and hear things in your mind. That's what it is."

"No, of course not!" Devin protested. "It's just what's there, it's not made up." He looked from one to the other. "Don't you see it too?"

"You don't understand, do you?" Kit said. Frisker shifted in her arms and she gripped him tighter. "We don't hear or feel anything when we look at the stars."

"Color is just color!" Malloy burst out. "Sound is just sound, taste is just taste; shapes don't have feelings, and feelings don't have shapes! But it's like you've got them all twisted and tangled.

"It sounds kind of cool, though," he added kindly.

"There! You said it sounded cool," Devin argued, "So you do feel sounds . . ."

Malloy shook his head. "Just a figure of speech, Strange Boy."

"I thought everyone saw things the same way," Devin said in a low voice. "I didn't know I was different."

"It's like a secret power!" Kit said, very excited. "Only, secret powers have to be useful, like X-ray vision or invisibility. What's the use of hearing colors and feeling noises if—"

She was interrupted by the sound of rustling. It was coming from a bush on the other side of the post. The children froze. In the sudden silence, the rustling came again. A cautious nose and pair of long ears appeared between the leaves and then, after a second or two, a small hare hopped into view, looked around, lifted a long back leg, and gave itself a good scratch.

Frisker leaped out of Kit's arms.

"Frisker, no!"

The puppy bounded forward, past the post, barking at the top of its tiny lungs. The hare vanished. Kit ran forward a few steps. She was almost at the post now.

"He went through!"

"Doesn't mean you can too," Luke said in a sharp voice. "Don't go a single step closer."

"Please, Frisker," Kit begged. She dropped to her knees. The dog looked at her, barked again, and raced back. "Good boy!" Kit cried, but Frisker swerved and tore past her, hurtling through the undergrowth in high excitement.

"What if he goes back past the posts again? I'll lose him," Kit wailed.

Ansel was standing by himself a few feet away. He had followed the others when they left the camp but had taken no part in the conversation, seeming uninterested in the posts or Devin's talk of stars. There was a dull look on his face, and he moved sluggishly, as if he was half asleep. Even the drama with Frisker had failed to rouse him, but now he lifted his head. The dog had appeared again, tearing down the path. He was four feet away when Ansel suddenly moved with instinctive, lightning speed. He leaped forward and dived head first toward the dog, catching him in his arms, his face smashing hard into the ground.

He scrambled to his feet, grinning. For a moment, he looked like his old self.

"You got him!" Kit cried, rushing forward. "That was amazing."

"Knew all that goalie practice would come in useful one day!" Ansel said.

"You're completely obsessed with soccer, you know that?" Luke said.

Ansel handed Frisker back to Kit. "You're hurt!" she cried. There was a large graze on Ansel's cheek. It was already oozing blood, and Kit rummaged for a handkerchief and wiped it gently. "It's nothing," Ansel said, although he held still while she looked after him, his eyes fixed on her face.

"You know what this means, don't you?" Luke said. "Frisker crossed the post without setting off the laser. That proves that it's not triggered by heat or a heartbeat. It must be wired to respond only to humans. Otherwise it'd be going off all the time when animals cross. I was thinking we could somehow fool it, but I don't see how we can stop being human."

Malloy stared at the ground and rubbed his head.

"It's a shame Frisker isn't trained in search and rescue," he said, glancing at the puppy. "He could search for someone to rescue us."

Malloy's face grew thoughtful. "Do you think any animal could get past the posts?" he asked Luke.

"Seems that way," Luke said. "Come on. We've got to get back. We don't want them to catch us wandering around."

They turned to leave.

"Hey!" Luke called. "Where are you going, Malloy? The camp's in the other direction."

"I just have to visit with Fulsome," Malloy said. He trotted off and disappeared down the path toward the farmyard.

The others walked back quickly, worried that they had been missed. But the camp was quiet. Two or three of the tents had lights on inside; the rest were dark. Devin was a little behind the others. Passing between two tents, one in darkness, the other lit from within, he heard low voices.

"She rode all day on her horse; it carried her far away to a castle by the sea . . ."

It was Roman's voice. Devin paused and heard Megs whisper, "What happened to the Princess of Fire then?"

"The Red Witch's armies were all around the castle and there was nothing to eat," Roman replied. "The Princess of Fire got very hungry. In the end she only had one sandwich left."

"That's real bad."

"Yes, it was. She decided to eat one half of the sandwich the first day and then one half of that the next. At last she was down to a single crumb that couldn't be cut in half no matter how small the knife she used."

"And then she was rescued?"

"Yes. The Black King came and fought all the armies. Nobody could stop him. He saved her."

"You're good at stories, Roman. Really good."

"I used to tell them to my little sister."

"She was lost . . ."

"Yes." Roman's voice was suddenly fierce. "But you won't be. I won't let it happen to you."

Devin suddenly felt uncomfortable about eavesdropping and continued on to his own tent. He crawled inside and found Ansel already asleep. Luke lay wide-eyed, his hands clenched into fists on his sleeping bag.

"Did you see Malloy?" he whispered.

"No."

"I wish he'd come back," Luke muttered. "He was upset about the posts. Not many people can tell when Malloy's upset. But I can. I know him. If I could just figure out how those posts operate . . ." His voice trailed off.

Devin closed his eyes and thought of Roman and Megs and the armies of the Red Witch and the broad back of his grandfather, knee deep in the meadow, cutting hay for Glancer. Then he slept, deeply and without dreams, only stirring slightly when Malloy entered the tent sometime later.

"That pig's a genius, I tell you," Malloy told him. "Fulsome will get us out."

But Devin had fallen back asleep again.

Thirteen

DEVIN WOKE EARLY. There was a thin film of dew on the outside of the tent. He stared at it carefully. It made the tent fabric glitter a bit, he thought, but perhaps he was the only one who saw it that way. It also made a ticking sound, which he felt on the back of his hands, but again, he didn't know if that was normal or not. Since the conversation about the stars, everything he saw and heard was suddenly up for question. How strangely everyone had looked at him! But he knew they were telling the truth. Hadn't the Administrator told him he was unusual? He'd been feeling too sick at the time to pay real attention. But she'd said he was one in ten million and she'd used a word for it, something scientific. Devin didn't remember what it was. Luke would probably know, but Devin didn't want to ask him. He didn't want to be one in ten million.

It made him feel lonely.

His thoughts were interrupted by the sound of Mrs. Babbage clapping her hands.

"Time to wake up! Rise and shine, everyone!"

"What the heck?" Malloy grunted in outrage, burrowing deeper into his sleeping bag.

"Everyone up! I have a special announcement." There was a flustered edge to Mrs. Babbage's voice, and Devin crawled over to the tent flap and stuck out his head. Around him, other bewildered children were starting to emerge, their hair tangled from sleep. Mrs. Babbage stood by the remains of the campfire, waving her arms in anxiety.

"Everyone up!"

In a little while, they were all standing around her, blinking and rubbing their eyes.

"I have a special announcement," Mrs. Babbage repeated. "The special announcement is that the Administrator has a special announcement. She wants to see all of you at once. You have half an hour to clean yourselves up. I want teeth brushed and clothes clean! She won't be pleased if you look untidy. Hurry now! Hurry!"

◆ ◆ ◆

By eight o'clock, they'd gathered in the courtyard, buzzing with chatter and questions. The staff members had assembled as well. Devin had been right, there were many more of them working at the Home than it seemed. The Administrator's announcement must be really momentous, he thought, to make them stop work like that.

All eyes were fixed on the tower. Mrs. Babbage was hovering by the door, frantically smoothing her hair and adjusting her cardigan.

The door opened and everyone fell silent.

The Administrator was wearing a suit so sharp and white that the light seemed to bounce clean off her. The suit had no visible buttons or pockets, and the lapels were broad, spreading like wings against her chest. She held herself stiff, as if gripped by great excitement.

"Late last night I had news of the utmost importance. We are about to receive a visit." Her hands were pressed together almost as if she was praying. "In the history of the Home, it has never happened before. It is an honor of the highest kind."

"What's she talking about?" Kit whispered in Devin's ear.

"An honor!" the Administrator repeated. Her voice rose. "We are about to receive a visit from none other than Gabriel H. Penn himself. Inventor, founder, and president of this home!"

Mrs. Babbage's hand shot up and covered her mouth. Murmurs filled the courtyard.

The Administrator waited for her news to sink in, then held her hands up for silence.

"My father must have the best experience possible. His visit must be perfect in every single way." There was an edge to her voice that held everyone's attention. "The grounds will be groomed down to the last blade of grass," she continued, addressing the staff. "Surfaces will be wiped and repainted if necessary. All trash will be removed. Windows will be washed. Every floor will be swept and every piece of glass and cutlery polished. The Home must look like a paradise."

She paused. "There is no dirt in Paradise. There is no untidiness."

She turned her focus on the children.

It was so quiet in the courtyard now that not a single whisper or rustle could be heard. Even the flock of birds above the tower, disturbed, perhaps, by the unusual size of the crowd below, had fallen completely silent.

"You will be perfect in dress and perfect in manners. My father does not wish to see brawling children and he does not wish to see crying children. Above all, he does not wish to see dirty children. No scabs, sores, or runny noses. Clean, washed faces, and clean, washed hands and—"

She was interrupted by a soft sound coming from the far side of the courtyard. It began as a snuffling and grew to a series of throaty grunts. The Administrator paused abruptly and frowned. The grunting came louder and more eager, then rose to a crescendo of snorts and squeals.

A fat, foul-smelling, and familiar shape charged headlong into the courtyard.

Fulsome's skin, normally the color of well-chewed bubble gum, was half hidden beneath a rich coating of mud, manure, and old leaves. A thistle dangled from his left ear. His legs dripped an oily substance, and there was a large stick wedged firmly in his mouth.

When he reached the center of the courtyard, he stopped, grunted, and looked around inquiringly, then began to turn excited circles on the spot.

In the dreadful silence, two things were instantly obvious. The first was that Fulsome had been rolling in the rankest, filthiest substances he could find. The second was that this rolling had only partly wiped away the words written large in black marker pen on his side. And what remained was clear enough for everyone to see.

CA . L OUT ARMY P . L ICE!

WE . R . PRIS . N . RS H . RE.

H . LP!!!!!!!!

For half a second, the Administrator, Mrs. Babbage, and the entire crowd of staff and children appeared completely paralyzed. Malloy's eyes bulged with horror. Luke's face froze midtwitch. Then all the children (and some of the staff) broke into a huge shout of laughter that nothing, not the Administrator's terrible glare nor Mrs. Babbage's flapping arms, could prevent.

"Oh Fulsome, Fulsome!" Malloy shrieked, bent double with laughter.

He stopped laughing, however, when the pig, tiring of showing off, took a firmer grip on the stick between his teeth and advanced confidently into the crowd.

"Oh no," he said, "Oh no, oh no, he's coming straight at me. She'll know I'm the one to blame."

He darted behind Devin and stood cowering, tugging on Devin's shirt in an effort to hide himself. But Fulsome had other things on his mind. Not long before, he had received a tasty treat for depositing a stick of roughly this length and weight at Luke's feet. He trotted through the crowd, which parted eagerly to let him pass.

He reached Luke, but Luke ducked away at the last moment and the stick fell to the ground at Ansel's feet instead.

"Ansel Fairweather!" The Administrator's voice cut through the hubbub like a knife.

"You are to report to my office at once!"

✦ ✦ ✦

They were meant to be tidying their rooms in readiness for the great Mr. Penn's visit, but Devin, Kit, Luke, and Malloy were too busy wondering what had happened to Ansel to do much work. After issuing her order, the Administrator had turned on her heel and disappeared into the tower, and Ansel, with the eyes of the crowd fixed pityingly on him, had trailed in after her. The children dispersed, and a staff member, still grinning, led Fulsome away.

"Bet they hose him down," Malloy commented. "He hates to be washed. It isn't natural for a pig, you know."

"What were you thinking, pulling a stunt like that?" Kit asked.

"It was such a genius idea," Malloy said. "After you'd gone back to the tents last night I went to the pigsty and took Fulsome out and I wrote that rescue note on his body. Even though he's little, there's a lot of room on Fulsome's body. He's chubby, you know.

"Not fat," he added hastily, "just nicely chubby."

Kit rolled her eyes.

"I led him to where we'd been sitting, near the posts," Malloy continued. "I looked him straight in the eye and I told him to go fetch. But I meant fetch help, not an old stick. I should have been more specific, I guess. I mean, even Fulsome can't read minds.

"One little word," he mourned, "between triumph and disaster . . ."

"You really think that if you'd told him to fetch help, Fulsome would have come galloping back with a rescue team?" Kit asked.

"Something like that, yeah."

"You're a moron, you know that?"

Malloy slumped forward, his head in his hands. "I should go, shouldn't I? I should go and own up and say it was me. It's not right for Ansel to take the blame."

Devin didn't know how to answer. It was awful thinking of Ansel being punished for something Malloy had done, but he didn't want to say that.

"I'd go like a shot," Malloy said, "except I'm too much of a coward. I'm more chicken than chicken pot pie. I'm more chicken than fried chicken with a side of chicken. I'm more chicken—"

"Okay, okay," Kit said. "We get the point."

"I should go," Malloy repeated. "Do you think I should go? I really ought to go . . ."

✦ ✦ ✦

Whether Malloy would have owned up or not, it was already too late. Ansel had been sent to the Place. Perhaps it was a punishment, or perhaps it was simply his turn again. As usual, it was Vanessa who had all the information. She sat in the common room looking self-important. Devin noticed that she had undone the top two buttons of her shirt, perhaps in imitation of the Administrator. She fingered the neckline, showing off her marker-made red nails.

According to Vanessa, Ansel had been sent to the Place. But he hadn't gone willingly.

"You mean he put up a fight?" Luke asked.

Vanessa shook her head. It hadn't been like that. "It

was more like he went crazy," she said. "He yelled things nobody could understand and fell down and wouldn't get up. Two staff members had to pick him up and take him away."

Malloy hung his head and went very quiet. He trailed off to the farmyard in search of Fulsome, and nobody else felt in the mood for talking. Devin wandered by himself for a while. The Home had become a scene of frenetic activity in preparation for Gabriel Penn's visit. Staff members were everywhere. The lawn mowers were out in force, leaf-blowers blasted the pathways; buckets and mops filled the dining room; hedges were being trimmed, horses brushed, and gravel raked. The air was full of the smells of fresh paint, soapy water, and cut grass. But the children themselves were stiller than ever. They moved listlessly, fearful of messing up their clothes, bewildered by the turn of events.

A small girl was swinging alone in the playground. Devin could see at once that she was in the Dream. She plunged back and forth, rising so high that her seat jerked in the air and hung slack-chained for a second before hurtling back down again. One of her shoes had fallen off. Her hair flew back, and her eyes were closed as if the swing was carrying her to a different world, a place so full of joy that she would stay there forever if she could. Apart from the heavy, rhythmic creak of the swing, there was no sound.

Jared was sitting alone on one of the benches by the carousel. Devin stared at him curiously. Nobody seemed to know Jared very well. They always referred to him just as "the boy with the teddy bear," and sure enough, there it was, sitting beside him on the bench. Jared was a tall boy, but he had his knees up so his legs didn't touch the ground. As Devin passed by, Jared waved at him, then picked up the bear and made it wave too, waggling the bear's paw playfully. Spoiled, Devin thought with a stab of pity and fear. He waved quickly and hurried away.

It was early evening when he got back to the court-yard, and he stopped, astonished. The courtyard had always been an impressive area, but now it was trans-formed. An army of staff members must have been work-ing on it all day. The driveway had been raked—Devin could still see the lines in the gravel—and the expanded flower beds were an explosion of color. Torches had been planted all around the open area, and moths flickered in their pools of light, and the curved walls of the tower were striped with twisted shadow. It looked beautiful, Devin thought. Almost magical.

As he stood there, a car pulled up. It was different from the car he'd arrived in, far larger, with a sleek sil-ver ornament on the hood, in the shape of an eagle. In the same instant, almost as if she had been waiting be-hind the tower door, the Administrator appeared on the threshold.

She had changed her clothes. Instead of her usual severe skirt and shirt, she wore a dress, pale blue and floaty. The pretty, rather girlish barrette pinned in her hair made her whole face look softer. She stepped forward and then stood waiting, her arms by her side. The car stopped and the front door opened and a man got out.

Devin held his breath. Was this the famous Gabriel Penn?

He was wearing a navy jacket with gold buttons and had a cap on his head. Not Penn, Devin thought. Just his driver; Penn must be still in the car.

Devin was too far away to hear. He stepped a little closer, keeping to the shadows. The Administrator said something and the driver shook his head. "I've been instructed . . . ," Devin heard him say, and then, ". . . purely a business visit . . ."

The Administrator glanced at the darkened windows of the car: ". . . a meal," she said, "all prepared . . . I was expecting . . ."

The driver shook his head again and spread his hands. He turned and got back into the car and in a second it was moving away toward the adult accommodations on the other side of the courtyard.

For a second or two, the Administrator simply stood there, watching it leave. Then she turned and Devin got a glimpse of her face, lit by the torches. Was it pain and disappointment that he saw? Was it rage?

It was impossible to tell. Her face was as blank as a slammed door.

Devin knew she couldn't see him, but her gaze seemed to find him as he shrank back against the dark wall.

I need you to be healthy, Devin.

He hurried back to his room and lay down on his bed, hugging his pillow, his insides hollowed out by dread.

I'm saving you for something special.

Fourteen

DEVIN COULDN'T SLEEP, AND after a while, he stopped trying. He sat, fully dressed, on the edge of his bed, watching as dawn crept over the sky. There was a tiny knock on the door.

"I'm the messenger," Karen said.

Devin nodded.

Karen twisted her hands together. "I'm sorry," she said. "I'm so sorry."

"You don't have to apologize. It's not your fault."

"I know. It's just that I'm always the messenger. It makes me feel . . ."

"It's okay," Devin said. "I'll be fine. Look out for Kit for me, will you?"

He left the room and went downstairs. The courtyard was empty. There was still dew on the grass, the faintest trace of moisture. It would be gone soon, when the sun rose. Devin looked up into the clear blue sky, wondering suddenly what it had been like to live in a world where clouds were common, everyday things. Where all kinds of plants grew without any help and there was always hay for the horse and grain for the chickens. It hadn't been as easy as that on the farm—they'd had to work for everything—but it had been better there. A pocket of richness, his grandfather had called it. There were seasons on the farm; spring brought a scattering of flowers in the hedgerow, and autumn, color to the trees. And one January morning, when he was very small, his grandfather had woken him up to show him a miracle: a glittering sheet of ice, paper thin, on the top of a bucket of water by the back door.

The farm was different from the outside, hidden and protected. It was as if it had been forgotten by time itself and simply left to its own blessed devices. Perhaps there were other spots like it, but Devin did not know of them. And whatever happened at this place, however confused his mind and terrible the dreams, he would hold on to the memory of the farm. A pocket of richness, the one safe place in all the world.

Mrs. Babbage was at the door of the tower.

"You're to report to the East Building," she said.

She meant the Place, of course. He followed her down the path, around the field with the small hill, and up toward the recreation hall and the turning with the strange, twisted trees. She didn't say anything to him as they walked. He thought perhaps that dim as she was, she understood he was afraid and felt a little sorry for him.

The entrance to the Place was open, and they went inside.

It was just as Luke had described it. The walls were white and shining and there was a room with nothing but screens and monitors and glass panels and a staff member in a white coat who led him to a chair without saying anything. The Administrator was there. He saw her at the back of the room behind one of the glass panels, looking intently at something, her hand held up as if to say "wait." Then she murmured something into a black button in front of her mouth and her hand came down.

Devin didn't see the needle going into his arm. He barely even felt it.

◆ ◆ ◆

He was awake, he felt almost sure of it; but he didn't know where he was. The pieces wouldn't fall into place. There was a ceiling above and light coming in and the vague shapes of furniture around him, but none of it fit together.

He didn't know where he was, but he felt that he should know.

Even worse, he didn't know who he was—his name, his age, his past, or his future. These were basic things—the most basic things of all—but they simply wouldn't come to him. Yet they felt very close, like words stuck on the tip of his tongue or a familiar tune whose notes refused to play. He was someone; everyone was someone unless they were dead. Was he dead? Was this what death was like? Not knowing who or how or even what you were?

A crack had opened in the universe, and he was falling through empty space without a single memory to clutch onto.

I am someone! I am someone! Help me!

Panic engulfed him, and for several moments he lay paralyzed while his mind whirled, battered by fear and confusion like a bird beating its wings against the bars of a cage. In a little while he became aware of a sound, a low, rasping noise like air squeezed through ancient, leaking bellows.

It was his own breath.

It sounded that way because his body hurt so much. He was not dead, then, he thought. Surely the dead didn't feel such pain. He was lying in a bed under a single white sheet, but it felt as though there was an iron board pressing down over the whole length of him. His throat was dry, his muscles ached, and all the joints in his body felt locked, as if they'd been tightened by invisible screws.

He turned his head and saw that the room he was in was high up; he could see fields through the window and something that glittered as it turned, catching the sun. He could tell by the light that it was midmorning. On the other side of the room were two doors. One was half open, and he could just see the edge of a bathroom seat and the side of a small sink. Apart from a table by the bed and a single chair, very large and comfortable looking, the room was empty.

There was the sound of keys and the door to the room suddenly opened. A woman came in. He felt sure he knew her, but equally sure he had never seen her before in his life. She had a pinched-looking face and was carrying a tray with a glass of clear liquid. He managed to raise his head slightly. As he did so, the pillows rose up behind him with a small hissing sound so that in a few seconds he was half-propped up with his neck and shoulders supported.

"Where am I?" he said with difficulty. His voice sounded odd in his ears, although he didn't know why.

"Right where you're meant to be," the woman said irritably. She came over and put the glass of liquid on the bedside table and went out of the room again without looking at him.

He stared at the glass. He was very thirsty. He lifted his hand and reached for it. There appeared to be a large gold ring on his middle finger. He stared at it stupidly for a second or two, then grasped the glass and drank it down.

Almost immediately, most of his pain seemed to ebb away. He sighed, his breath rattling in his throat. His fear retreated too. It was still there, but only slightly, a shadow at the edge of things. His thoughts became muffled; the walls of the room lost their sharpness and grew vague and spongy. He dozed.

The light changed and changed again. He dreamed.

He dreamed he was on an empty plain. No trees grew there or plants of any kind. The sky was low and hard, curved like the inside of a tin mug turned upside down to catch a beetle. A boy was sitting on the ground a little way ahead with his back to him and the hood of his jacket up. He couldn't see the boy's face, but a terrible misery radiated from him, a stink of desperate sorrow and regret beyond all power to comfort. He didn't want to keep walking, but he couldn't help it. He was close to the boy now, close enough to hear him crying.

He left me, he left me . . .

There were tears running down his own cheeks; grief clutched his heart.

It's too late, too late, too late . . .

The boy's small shoulder in its blue jacket was just below him. He reached out his hand.

◆ ◆ ◆

He woke up and he was back again in the dream of the room with the single chair. Someone had come in and left a tray of food for him.

The food looked strange. A single fried egg lay on a white plate. A tiny tomato that had been scooped out to form a bowl lay to the right of the egg. To the left, three slices of mushroom had been placed in a fan arrangement, each slice overlapping its neighbor with perfect regularity. He stared at it dully. It didn't seem like a meal that had been cooked in the ordinary way, he thought. It was more like something that had been put together with tweezers by a person holding their breath.

He ate in a daze, without tasting.

The light changed. It grew dark outside.

He thought he was awake and standing by the window but he must have been asleep, because there was a man outside looking in at him and he knew that was impossible. The room was high up. The man would have to be fifty feet tall. He was an old man with cheekbones as sharp as knives, and he stared at him through the glass.

"I'm dreaming," he cried to himself in terror. "I'm dreaming!"

The lights went off and the man went away.

Time stood still and then suddenly passed. "Where am I?" he asked the woman with the pinched face. "Please . . . tell me my name."

"Wouldn't you like to know?" she said, handing him

another glass of liquid. "Drink it up now like a good boy . . ." She was smiling, her whole face lit up with satisfaction.

"That's it," she said. "Drink it all up and have a nice little sleep."

He didn't want to sleep. The boy would be there, waiting for him. He didn't want to see the boy or touch him. But wanting had nothing to do with it. He slept and dreamed of the empty plain again. There was a trail of small footprints in the dust. They ran across the ground with skips and hops and he followed their path, his own feet dragging, his heart flooded with anguish.

The footprints ended and the boy was there. His head was down, hidden by the hood of his jacket, and his shoulders twitched as he sobbed.

He left me. He hasn't come back.

"Who left you?" he said, and touched the boy's shoulder.

The boy turned his head and looked at him and he staggered back in horror.

He had the wrong face. Not the innocent face of a child, but that of an old man, the old man who had been looking in through the window. The same sagging, pitted skin, the same pale, watery eyes. And he was staring at him with a look as cold and distant as the stars.

He tried to scream, but for a long moment, no sound came. Then, like bats bursting from a cave, his shrieks came thick and fast and seemed to have no end.

Fifteen

DEVIN WOKE IN HIS bed at the Home, under the quilt of patchwork stars. For a second or two he could barely believe it, and then he was overcome by relief. He pulled his knees up to his chest and hugged himself as hard as he could. He was back, he was safe. He was himself again.

But the feeling of the dream wouldn't quite go away, and after the relief passed, a strange unease came over him. He felt mysteriously changed. It was as if someone had crept into his home while he was away and used everything and moved everything around and then, just before he got back, returned them to almost the right places. Almost, but not quite. Devin couldn't identify what it was, but he knew something was different.

Tears rose in his eyes and ran down his face. They

tasted of dark-blue dust. Did everyone taste tears that way? It didn't seem to matter anymore. Nothing he felt or did seemed to matter. Before going to the Place, he'd told himself he would hold on to the memory of his farm, whatever happened. But he hadn't been able to. A great feeling of helplessness washed over him, and for a little while he lay in his bed without moving, simply crying.

He heard a scuffling at the door and wiped his eyes quickly. Luke was outside, with Malloy and Kit.

"Welcome back," Luke said. "We missed you."

"Fulsome was all sad!"

"Frisker too," Kit said gently, and held out the puppy for him to pet.

Devin looked from one to the other, so glad to see them he thought he might cry again.

"Thanks," he said. "Thanks. I missed you too."

✦ ✦ ✦

They sat down and told him what had been happening while he'd been in the Dream. There wasn't much to report except that Megs had succeeded in setting fire to her doll's hair, using one of the courtyard torches, and after that, all the torches had been removed. The main news was that since her father's visit, the Administrator had introduced a number of annoying new rules. For a start, there was now a dress code.

"We have to wear socks," complained Kit. "And if you have long hair you have to keep it tied back."

"And you have to keep your room tidy," Malloy chimed in. "They come around and check."

They'd also heard from Vanessa that the Administrator wasn't happy with the group activities. Vanessa claimed to have heard the Administrator lecturing Mrs. Babbage about arranging a better one, a scavenger hunt with objects for the kids to find all over the Home. Since then, Mrs. Babbage had been scurrying around frantically, trying to set it up.

"Complete waste of time," Luke commented. "It'll be pathetic . . ."

At lunch Devin was glad to find he was hungry. He heaped his plate with macaroni and cheese and sat down with the others. He didn't want to talk much. It was enough just to sit there and listen to the chatter.

"Mac 'n' cheese is such a useless food," Missie announced.

"You don't have to eat it," Kit informed her.

"That's not the point. The point is . . . Karen, why are you sitting so close? I can't move my elbow . . ."

"Sorry about that, sorry." Karen hunched her shoulders and shifted away.

"The point is that it's boring. Mac 'n' cheese is boring. It's a boring, boring food." Finding no agreement, Missie glanced at Pavel sitting silently at the other end of the table.

"It's boring, right, Pavel?"

Pavel, of course, said nothing.

"Can't you say anything at all?"

Malloy flicked a drip of cheese at Missie. "Sure he can," he said. "He's just waiting until there's something worth saying."

Missie pushed some food into her mouth with an angry gesture. "All I'm saying is that it's dull." She chewed and swallowed. "It's the food equivalent of watching paint dry. No, it's worse than that. It's the food equivalent of a jigsaw puzzle, one of those huge ones with nothing but sky." Her voice quivered with indignation. "Or nothing but sky and windmills."

Devin wondered why nobody told her to be quiet. He could tell she was annoying everyone. But perhaps Missie's endless grouching was simply her way of getting through the day, her way of surviving. And perhaps the others knew this, whether they realized it or not. He gazed at the faces around the table.

Look at the way Malloy stuck up for Pavel just a minute ago, he thought. Everyone's got a weakness, but we cover for each other and we make allowances, for Pavel, for Missie, for poor Jared who wants to stay a little boy forever . . .

He suddenly saw that they were a team. And that he would never feel lonely again, because he was one of them now.

Mrs. Babbage made her pattering way to the food table.

"If I could have everyone's attention," she bleated. "Attention . . . everyone . . . ?"

It was a while before the chattering died down, but finally there was quiet in the room. Mrs. Babbage looked around and gave a big smile. "I have wonderful news to share with you," she said. "Ansel Fairweather has been adopted!"

There was a second of silence and then a sigh rippled around the room, half of pleasure, half of envy.

"In a little while," Mrs. Babbage continued, "you will be able to see the photograph of Ansel with his new parents in the common room. I'm just on my way now to pin it up."

Someone started clapping, and in a second all the children had joined in. Devin glanced at Kit. She was clapping harder than anyone else, her lips bunched up and her eyes shining.

✦ ✦ ✦

The others had finished lunch. Only Devin and Luke were left at the table. Without being asked, Vanessa came over and sat down with them.

"You were weird," she announced, staring at Devin.

"What do you mean?"

"In the Dream. You were so immature."

Devin felt his hands begin to tremble.

"Hey!" Luke interrupted. "You're not supposed to talk about it. It's the rule."

"It's not my rule," Vanessa retorted. "I've got my own rules."

"What . . . what did I do?" Devin faltered.

Luke gave him a nudge in the ribs. "Don't ask!"

Vanessa smiled a small, superior smile. "You touched everything and you smiled and your breath went all gaspy and you stared at the sky like you'd never seen it before."

"I did?"

"You licked the grass. You ate some dirt. I saw you!"

Luke stood up suddenly and shoved his dinner tray at her. "Shut up! Shut your mouth!" he yelled.

The tray slid across the table and hit Vanessa in the chest. She stood up at once, brushing herself off in an exaggerated way.

"You are so pathetic," she said.

"I don't know what's wrong with her," Luke said as she marched away. "I don't know why she's so mean. It's like she thinks she's better than any of the kids here and doesn't want anything to do with any of us.

"Don't pay any attention to her," he added. "Don't listen to a word she says."

Devin nodded, but it was hard not to feel disturbed. His uneasiness of the morning had returned, seasoned with a new feeling of shame. It wasn't his fault that he'd acted "weird," as Vanessa had put it, but he couldn't help wishing he'd been able to have more control over himself.

◆ ◆ ◆

It was evening. Devin and Malloy were at the gates of the large meadow, watching the horses and talking. Malloy was wondering whether it would be possible to get past the laser posts on horseback if the rider lay very low. That way, the posts might fail to detect the presence of a human. Devin thought it sounded far too risky, although he had his eye on the largest of the horses, a piebald mare that looked strong and eager. She reminded him a little of Glancer.

"I've gotta get out of here, I've just gotta," Malloy said. "My mom and dad, they're not very . . . Well, to be honest, I don't think they'll find me without some help. Luke's sure they will and I always agree with him, but I kind of only do that because I can tell it cheers him up. The truth is, my mom and dad couldn't find their way out of a paper bag."

Devin didn't say anything. He watched the sun dip behind the trees and the golden rumps of the horses and the long, whistling grass.

"Luke says there's a control box in the Administrator's office," Malloy went on.

"He told me about that," Devin said.

"She wears the key for it around her neck. I bet it controls the laser posts." Malloy paused. "We'd have to get that key, but how? And even if we did, Luke says for sure there's a code we'd need to know before we could disarm the posts . . ." His voice trailed off.

Devin had never seen him so serious. He'd thought Malloy couldn't be serious to save his life.

"Guess I'm just gonna have to fly out of here," Malloy said, grinning suddenly. "Have to lose some weight, though." He patted his stomach. "Never going to get liftoff with this belly.

"I tell you what," he went on. "When I do get out of here, I'm taking that bird with me."

"Bird?"

"That parrot of hers." Malloy clenched his fists. "Poor thing. Poor tatty old thing. Why does she have to treat it like that?"

"She hates failure," Devin said. "She told me that when I saw her on my second day here. I think she keeps the bird to scare us. To show us that she's never going to stop punishing anything or anyone who disappoints her."

"Nah," Malloy said. "I think she just likes hurting things. When I get out of here, I'm taking that bird and I'm going to the jungle where it came from and I'm letting it go free. Won't that be great?"

Devin nodded, smiling.

"I can just see it now," Malloy said. "Me and that bird in the jungle . . . all the animals everywhere . . . kind of like heaven."

"But where is the jungle?" Devin asked.

Malloy paused in his reverie. "Not sure," he admitted. "But wherever it is, I'm gonna find it."

✦ ✦ ✦

Malloy had left, and Devin stood alone by the gate, watching the sunset. He was so still, the piebald mare grew curious and wandered over, pushing her head toward him. Devin stepped onto the first rung of the gate and leaned over to pet her nose. She was wearing her bridle, and without thinking, moving automatically, he took it in one hand, climbed to the top of the gate, and slipped quickly and easily onto her back. She startled slightly and half wheeled, and he leaned forward to pat her neck, whispering to her. He nudged his heels against her sides and she took off at once, with a long stride that in seconds had become a gallop.

They raced around the large meadow, the wind whipping Devin's hair. Faster and faster they went. He thought if he went fast enough he could outrun the memory of his bad dreams and that terrible word *spoiled* and all that it meant. And for a while, with the blurred trees roaring as they flashed past and the sky ringing golden and his heart thundering to the beat of the mare's hooves on the dry earth, for a little while it really felt as though he might.

Sixteen

THERE WAS A NEW sense of tension in the Home. Perhaps it was all the recent rules or perhaps it was the sight of the Administrator herself. Before, she had mostly kept to herself in the tower, but now she seemed to be everywhere, checking the work of the gardeners, inspecting the kitchen, circling the courtyard with a narrowed eye as if judging the angle of the buildings themselves. She had also started carrying Darwin around on her shoulder. Darwin looked worse than ever, more like a clot pulled out of a filthy drain than a bird. Perhaps, since her father's visit to the Home, it was even more important to remind everyone what would happen if they failed her. Or perhaps Malloy was right and she simply enjoyed tormenting the creature.

Mrs. Babbage tagged along behind. She kept nodding,

her hands fluttering with anxiety as the Administrator issued orders.

"This is not up to standard, Babbage!" the Administrator said, her words carrying the length of the dining hall. "I simply won't have it. Sort it out!"

Kit had also changed since Devin had been in the Dream. She was quieter, her fierceness turned inward, and Devin noticed that she no longer asked as many questions as before. He found her in her room the next day before breakfast. She was lying on her stomach on the floor. Arranged around her were items from the dollhouse. There were a lot of them; Devin had no idea that she'd stolen such a vast hoard.

In addition to the tea service, her collection now included three lamps; a table; a vase of flowers; a harp which, though tiny, still had all its strings; a perfectly formed, real crystal chandelier; two oil paintings no larger than a fingernail; a desk; a trunk with a minuscule lock; a four-poster bed; a violin with a bow the size of a needle; and eight chairs with velvet seats and curly wooden backs.

Kit was staring raptly at something in the palm of her hand when Devin came in. She held it out for him to see. It was a tiny box with a glass lid, containing several rows of real shells, none larger than the head of a pin.

"Can you believe it?" she said. "It's a collection inside a collection . . ."

Devin wondered why she'd taken so many things. After all, she could have played with them in the dollhouse whenever she wanted. He sat down on the bed, rubbing his head. He hadn't slept much the night before.

"Kit," he said. "When you . . . came back . . . did you worry you'd have the same dreams? That they'd follow you even though you were back to normal?"

Kit shrugged slightly. She lowered her head so her chin was resting on the floor and her eyes were level with the dollhouse furniture.

"My granddad said if you want to dream of something good, you just think about it really hard before you fall asleep. I've been trying to do that, but I'm worried it won't work and instead I'll dream about—"

Kit interrupted him. "You know what's amazing? If you get down low like this and kind of squint your eyes, you can almost imagine all this stuff is life size. You can see how it would be if it was real, if you lived in a house with it all around you. And nobody would punish you if it got lost or broken because there was so much of it."

"I guess so," Devin said uncertainly. He looked down at his hands. "It's just that if I can't stop thinking about the bad dreams, then I'll dream them again, won't I? Even if I'm trying to think about good stuff like the farm and Granddad . . ."

Kit jerked to her knees abruptly. "Stop talking about

it, then!" Her face was pinched with anger. "The trouble with you is that you need to grow up!"

Devin stared at her. Kit got to her feet and smoothed her dress down, her hands agitated. "Sorry for telling the truth," she said furiously, catching sight of his wounded expression. "But it's not about sitting around feeling sorry for yourself. It's about doing what it takes."

"What it takes?"

"To get adopted."

"To maybe get adopted," Devin said.

"Why maybe? It happened to Ansel. You saw his photo, didn't you?"

Devin nodded. They had all been to the Common Room to look at the photo of Ansel. In the picture he was sitting at a table with two women who, although old, were still beautiful. One had silvery hair that fell to her shoulders in luxurious waves. The other was wearing a white skirt and held a tennis racquet. Behind them, slightly out of focus, there was a shelf with what looked like several trophies, large and golden.

Lucky Ansel, Devin had thought. He's gone to a sporting family.

But as Devin had looked from Ansel's face to the faces of the women and back again, something tugged at the back of his mind, a vague sense of oddness. He frowned—he couldn't decide what it was. Perhaps it was simply that the last time Devin had seen Ansel, he'd seemed so dazed and shattered. But in the picture there was no sign of it. He looked strong and happy again.

"It happened to Ansel," Kit repeated. "And it will happen to us too. But you've got to get tough, Devin. You've got to do what it takes."

◆ ◆ ◆

Mrs. Babbage was in the dining room at breakfast with pencils and paper and a bunch of cloth bags slung over her arm. She stood by the door with a frazzled look on her face.

"I've worked very hard on this . . . it's all set up . . . ," she muttered as she distributed the bags and papers.

Malloy was busy demolishing a plateful of French toast as Mrs. Babbage passed by and handed him a bag.

"Thanks, Mrs. Cabbage!"

She stopped uncertainly. "I don't think I heard that," she said.

Malloy chewed and swallowed. He grinned. "I just wanted to say thanks, but my mouth was full. Sorry to be rude, Mrs. Cabbage."

Mrs. Babbage looked even more uncertain. She glanced around. Luke, Devin, and Kit were staring at her with completely straight faces.

"My hearing must be going. Never mind," she said, and went on her way. Devin couldn't help grinning, although he thought it was perhaps a little cruel to mock Mrs. Babbage. She couldn't help it if she wasn't very clever.

Luke was looking at the paper Mrs. Babbage had handed him. It was a list of all the things they were supposed to go find on the scavenger hunt.

"Three stars, a four-leaf clover," he read. "Five things with eyes (humans not included!), six blue objects that are also circular, something beginning with the letter *Q*, something that rattles, three yellow things that are rectangular or square . . ." He groaned. "This is going to take hours."

He was interrupted by the clap of Mrs. Babbage's hands as she called for order.

"You will do the scavenger hunt in pairs," she announced. "Partners have been assigned. I have the list here."

Devin's heart sank. He knew it was too much to expect he would be paired with one of his friends, and sure enough, he wasn't.

"Luke and Karen," Mrs. Babbage announced, going down the list. "Malloy and Megs, Missie and Pavel, Kit and Jared . . ."

He was going to get a kid in the Dream, he knew it. A whole day spent trying not to look at or hear or even notice some kid acting strange. Now that he'd been in the Dream himself, now that he'd gone through the whole awful thing, he could barely glance at someone else going through it without feeling sick. Please, anyone but a kid in the Dream, he thought. Anyone . . .

It wasn't a kid in the Dream. It was worse.

"Devin and Roman," Mrs. Babbage said.

✦ ✦ ✦

Everyone trailed out of the dining room except for Roman and Devin.

"You going to carry the bag or should I?" Roman said.

"You carry your own bag," Devin said.

Roman pushed back his chair and stood up. He looked at his watch.

"Better get started. It's going to take a while."

"Not really. It's obvious where everything is."

Curiosity flickered in Roman's pale eyes.

"Are you going to be like this all day?" he asked.

"Like what?"

"Like you'd rather die than talk to me." He paused. "I know what the other kids call me. They call me Traitor. Is that what you call me too?"

Devin had heard Roman called that and worse. The kids at the Home shared a passion in their dislike of him. Vanessa never failed to stare at him as he passed, her eyes narrowing malevolently. Devin had seen one boy actually spit at him. Even Malloy joked about feeding him to Fulsome, though as Luke pointed out, Fulsome would probably turn up his snout in disgust. Nobody could forget that it was Roman who had lured them there with his talk of good food and endless play. The worst of it was that Roman himself knew what it was like to be in the Dream. He'd been there himself. Vanessa had told Devin all about it.

"Roman's been five times. That's what I heard," she had said. "I keep count."

"Of everyone?"

She nodded. "Yes. Five times for Roman. Megs is fourteen times. That's because she looks so babyish."

"Really?"

"Oh, yes, didn't you know? The younger you look, the more times you have to go."

She paused, brushing her curled hair away from her face with a careful, ladylike gesture. "I seem older than I am," she told him. "Don't you think so?"

Luke had wondered why Vanessa always acted so mean. Now Devin thought he knew.

"Yes," he said kindly. "Yes, a little."

"A lot," she corrected. "In fact, I don't look like a kid at all. I don't act like one, either."

Roman had been in the Dream five times. So he knew how bad it was. But he kept bringing kids back from the city. Maybe he'd made a deal with the Administrator, Devin thought. Maybe if he brought enough new kids in, he wouldn't have to go to the Place anymore himself.

In that case, he really was a traitor. Not that Devin would ever say it out loud.

He looked away. "I don't call you anything at all," he said truthfully.

Roman's mouth twisted. "No," he said. "No, you wouldn't. You're too good for that."

Devin wondered whether he was making fun of him, but Roman wasn't smiling.

"Come on," Devin said, a little roughly. "Let's get this over with." He looked at the list Mrs. Babbage had given him and then closed his eyes. It was easier to see the map in his head when his eyes were closed. He waited and sure enough, the colors and shapes swam into view, growing clearer as his mental gaze ranged over the intricate pattern of the Home. At last they were all in focus.

"There's a soccer ball with stars on it in the shed . . . ," he told Roman, "blue plates in the dining room . . . plus a blue Frisbee also in the shed, a pack of yellow playing cards in the common room on the shelf under the books . . . Needles have eyes, don't they? There are some in the drawer also in the common room."

Roman let his breath out in a soft whistle of surprise but said nothing.

After half an hour, although all the other kids were still searching, Devin and Roman had found almost everything on the list. The only thing left was the four-leaf clover. Roman said there was a big clump of them on the hill in the small meadow.

"I know because she told me once."

Devin knew without having to ask, who "she" was. No doubt "she" and Roman had many little cozy chats, he thought. He walked faster, longing to be done with the hunt and Roman's company.

There must have been thousands and thousands of four-leaf clovers growing in the clump on the top of the hill. In fact, there was nothing but four-leaf clovers there. Devin bent down and picked one and thrust it into his bag. Done. He turned to leave.

"She wanted them so she had them planted," Roman said in a low voice. He plucked a handful, closing his fist tight around the green sprigs. "Kind of misses the whole point of finding one, doesn't it?" He glanced at Devin. "Four-leaf clovers are only lucky because they're rare. Plant a whole clump and they're just weeds." His fist opened and the clovers fell.

"I'm going back," Devin said. "We've found everything."

"I was a bit like you once," Roman said abruptly. "People thought well of me. I used to go to school. It wasn't a great school but it had a baseball team."

Devin didn't know why Roman was telling him this or why he should stay to listen. But there was a strange look on Roman's face. At first Devin thought he was angry.

"I played catcher," Roman said in a tight, hard voice. "You know what a catcher is?"

Devin shook his head.

"The catcher has to have a lightning arm and an even faster mind," Roman said. "He has to know the whole game inside and out, and he can never relax because he's involved in every single play. The pitcher might get more attention, but it's the catcher who's the true leader. He's got everyone's back, and from where he stands, he can see the whole field."

He paused. "I was the best catcher that school had ever had."

He spoke so seriously and so sadly that Devin almost felt sorry for him.

"Why did you do it, then?" he said sharply. "Why did you become a traitor?"

Roman's face lost all expression. His pale eyes gazed blankly down the little slope.

"I guess everyone has their price," he said.

Seventeen

DEVIN AND KIT HAD been at the Home for nearly two weeks now, although it seemed much longer. The days blurred into each other and it was hard to keep track of the time. Some of the kids knew how long they had been there, others appeared to have lost all sense of the weeks and months. Luke didn't seem to think that anyone had been there much longer than a year, apart from Roman and Megs. Nobody knew when they'd arrived.

Nothing disturbed the monotony of the days except for the occasional group activity and visits to the Place, which Devin learned happened about once every two weeks or so. He wasn't expecting to have to go again for a while, so it came as a shock when he got the message barely four days after his last visit.

"Too soon," Luke said, looking worried. "Kids never have to go again that soon."

All the way to the Place, Devin kept the images of field and farmhouse tight in his mind. And as he allowed himself to be led to the chair to wait for his shot, he imagined himself in his favorite place of all, the barn. It was dark and sweet in there, the refuge of mice and small creatures. Up in the beams over the door, swallows made their nests. The walls were old, and sunlight sent a hundred golden threads through the chinks and cracks in the wood . . .

Devin closed his eyes as the needle went in.

I remember the barn. I am there, I am there.

But then he woke and his memories were gone. In their place was nothing but pain and confusion. He lay very still, crying silently, the tears dripping down the side of his face onto the pillow.

This time he didn't turn his head or speak when the woman came in with the drink that took away pain. She put it down on the bedside table.

"Down in the dumps are you?" she said. "Dear, oh dear."

He waited until she had left before reaching gratefully for the drink. His hands trembled. He twisted, trying to get a better grip on the glass, but his fingers were wet with tears and the glass slipped and fell, tumbling onto the floor, the liquid drenching the sheet and carpet.

He heard himself groan—a long, low, terrible sound.

He needed the drink. He couldn't endure another moment without it. He lifted his head from the pillow and called out to the woman, his voice reedy with panic.

"Help! Come back! I spilled it."

But nobody came.

After a long struggle, he managed to shift his legs over to the side of the bed. Slowly he sat up. A bolt of pain shot through him from the base of his spine, then ebbed as he gasped and panted. He rested his feet cautiously on the floor and swayed upright. He could see out the window. There were fields and buildings and a great number of birds wheeling in the sky. He rubbed his eyes. His fingers were sticky from the liquid that he'd spilled. He turned toward the door that led to the small bathroom.

It was hard to walk. He had to go carefully. His whole body felt as though it might break at the slightest misstep. Without the numbing effects of the painkiller, the pain was severe, but his mind also felt sharper. He found himself able to think and even form vague opinions. There was something wrong, for example, very wrong, with the way his feet moved. His head was too heavy; his arms seemed to dangle far below him. But he was too busy to pay these things more than passing attention.

He shuffled by slow degrees toward the bathroom

and stopped when he reached it, leaning against the door, out of breath with effort.

At the sink he reached out and turned on the tap. He lifted his head and stared at the wall above the sink. It was blank. Shouldn't there be something there? There was a bar of soap in a small dish by the side of the sink. He reached for it automatically. It smelled of something. He brought it up to his face, breathing in the scent.

A long sighing sound, a flash of blue—very bright and clean.

Smells good, doesn't it?

He reached for the name and like a miracle, he found it. Rosemary.

It helps improve your memory. A long time ago people used to place it in graves for remembrance.

The soap smelled of rosemary. And in an instant, like a door unlocked and suddenly thrown open, everything came back to him. It was just as if his grandfather had returned from the dead and was standing at his shoulder, his collar straight and his eyes calm. *You are Devin,* his grandfather said. *Wake up! Remember!*

In the same moment, he knew what was missing from the space above the sink.

It was a mirror.

Devin dropped the soap in shock. He lifted his hands and looked at them.

They were not his hands.

But he could feel the hands! He could feel the smear of soap on the tips of the fingers, a slight itch in the right palm, the way the ring—shaped like an eagle—chafed against the skin.

But they were not his hands. And these legs—long and bony; these dangling arms; this heart pattering weakly in his chest; this breath itself, coming in short, fearful gasps . . . None of it belonged to him. He brought his fingers up to his face and groped his cheeks frantically. All of it was unfamiliar, the features of somebody else, somebody old and weak.

He was dreaming, Devin told himself desperately. It was just another dream. But he knew it wasn't. It was too real and detailed to be a dream, and his body hurt too much. He staggered against the sink.

He didn't know how long he stood there, sick to his stomach, his senses reeling in confusion. What should he trust, his mind or this withered body? Where did he really exist?

You exist where I am, his grandfather answered. *In your memory, in your love. Remember when you were small and used to hold my hand to walk?*

Devin nodded. "Yes, I remember."

Hold it again. Hold on as long as you need to, Dev. I won't let you fall.

Devin closed his eyes and took a long, deep breath.

He was Devin. He used to live on a farm, and now he

lived at the Home for Childhood, where terrible things were done to kids . . . and where something terrible had just been done to him. There was an explanation and he would find it.

The tap was still running. He thrust his hands under the stream and splashed his face, shuddering at the feel of his slack and pitted skin. He wanted to wriggle away, out of this body, as ugly as a cuckoo in another bird's nest. But he forced himself to stay calm. He dried his face on a hand towel and tottered back into the main room.

He looked out the window and at once recognized the view. It was the Home, of course. There was the tower, the wheeling birds, and there was the carousel, still turning. He was in a room at the top of the Place. He'd never left it.

But that wasn't possible. Of course he'd left it! That's what happened at the Place: You went in and then you came out and for two days you were in the Dream. You didn't remember it, but everyone else could see you perfectly clearly . . .

Yet he was here. At least his mind was here, all his thoughts and memories and feelings.

Then who was the boy—the Devin—that was running around down there?

He breathed deeply, keeping the panic at bay, trying to think.

They've swapped us, he thought. Me and some old man. I have his body and he has mine.

It was the only explanation that made sense. No wonder they kept it a secret. The thought alone was enough to drive anyone half crazy. Devin reached his bed and saw the glass still lying on the floor where it had fallen. He bent painfully and picked it up and put it on the table. There was a large wet stain on the carpet where the drug had spilled. He tugged at the sheet on the bed, pulling down a corner to cover the stain, and then made his way to the large chair on the other side of the room. He sat down.

There was a rattle at the door and he closed his eyes, lolling his head as if lost in sleep. He had to act like he was in a daze, he thought. He had to look as if nothing unusual had happened.

He smelled food. It was the woman with a tray holding his lunch. He heard her place it heavily on the table.

"I dunno why they bother giving you this fancy stuff," she grumbled. "But the clients can't miss their creature comforts, even if they're not here to enjoy them."

He knew that voice! He half opened his eyes for a second. How could he not have recognized Mrs. Babbage before? But this was not the Mrs. Babbage he knew. Gone were the smiles and placating gestures. This Mrs. Babbage was hard and complaining.

"Wants everything perfect, she does," she muttered. "Worse than before, ever since *he* came . . ."

She leaned toward him, and he felt her breath against his cheek.

"Bon app-e-teet!" she said, drawing the word out with relish.

She's not stupid at all, Devin thought. Not even slightly dim. She was actually enjoying his suffering. It was the only fun she got in life.

He heard her footsteps going away and then the rattle of the door being locked. He glanced at his meal, an elaborate arrangement of baby carrots and delicately sliced meat. It smelled good, but Devin had no appetite. The thought of eating, of thrusting food down his throat into someone else's body, suddenly seemed almost disgusting.

He had to get out of the room. Kit had taught him to pick locks back in the city, using a piece of bent wire. Could he do it here? The thought made his heart pound weakly and he pressed his knotted hand against his chest, trying to still himself. There wasn't any wire in the room, nothing he could use. There was only the bed and the chair and the small table. The lights were even set into the ceiling.

Devin didn't know how long he sat there, sunk in dismay, his gaze fixed dully on the gray carpet. After a while a tiny object came into focus, something that lay half on the carpet and half off. He hadn't seen it before, but it was late afternoon now and the light had changed. The beams of sunlight coming in through the window were lower, and one of them had found the object where it lay in the shadows and made it glitter.

Devin leaned forward for a better look. He lifted himself out of the chair and with a great effort got to his knees and crawled over to the object.

It was a hairpin.

Mrs. Babbage, Devin thought as his hand closed eagerly over it. It must have fallen out of her bun on one of her trips to and fro.

It was harder than he thought to pick the lock. This wasn't because it was particularly difficult, but because his old hands shook so much. It was a while before he could steady them enough even to insert the pin into the lock, and then it took a good ten minutes of fiddling before he heard the click of the door coming free. He hauled himself to his feet, opened the door, and looked out cautiously.

He saw nothing but an empty corridor with white walls. A thin strip of gray wool carpet ran down the center, and there were three doors—all closed—on the same side as his room. At the end of the corridor was another door, larger and without a doorknob. Devin took a deep breath and stepped out into the hall.

His feet were bare. They were horrible to look at, huge blue-veined things with gnarled yellow toenails. But he was glad because having bare feet meant he could walk quietly. He crept along, keeping to the wall. When he got to the first door, he paused. He could hear something. He leaned his ear closer to the wood, listening. Someone inside was wailing very softly, with a sound as formless as the wind.

They have another kid in there, Devin thought. Someone else who's been swapped. He remembered his first sight of the place, how he'd seen something moving at the window. He'd thought it was a claw, but now he knew it wasn't. It was the hand of someone very old, pressed up against the glass . . .

He walked on past the other doors. When he got to the one without a doorknob at the end of the corridor, he paused and listened. But he couldn't hear anything. He pushed the door and it swung open. He was standing at the top of a flight of stairs. There were no windows. Instead, the staircase was bright with a cold, harsh light that cast no shadow. There was nowhere to hide if anyone came up the stairs toward him.

Devin took a firm grip on the stair rail and began slowly easing his way down.

✦ ✦ ✦

The stairs led to the ground floor. The corridors were wider down here, although equally white and clean looking. There were a great many doors leading into rooms that looked like offices. Devin shuffled along, not sure what he was looking for and desperately afraid he would be caught. He saw a door made of metal that was polished as bright as a mirror, and a wide lobby with chairs. Everything was lit with the same artificial light.

He passed a hallway that he recognized—it led to the room where he'd sat for his shot—and turned away hastily. Then, just ahead, he heard the sound of footsteps. Someone was coming around the corner, walking briskly. Without thinking, Devin pushed open a door to his left and ducked inside. He held his breath until he heard the footsteps pass by, and then glanced around to see where he was.

He was in a pleasant-looking room with a big vase of yellow roses on a low table and a lot of soft chairs. A large portrait of a man in a gray suit hung on the far wall, and a table in one corner held a variety of drinks and crystal glasses. A neat pile of magazines lay on the table, and Devin walked over to take a look.

Up close, he realized they were brochures, not magazines. He picked one up. There was a photograph on the cover. It was a picture of the Home, the large meadow with the courtyard and tower in the background, and a soft, sunny haze on the grass. In large letters above the photo, he read the words *An Introduction*.

Devin opened the brochure. Inside were more photos

of the Home: children playing on the go-carts and the climbing wall and a big close-up of one of the horses on the carousel, its wooden mane tossed back, its teeth bared.

Are you low? Are you bored? Devin read. *Have you lost heart?*

Has the passing of time sapped your strength and dulled your spirit?

We offer the solution!

Simply press RE-PLAY!

Devin turned the page.

WHAT IS RE-PLAY?

The Re-Play Treatment is a unique remedy for the depression of old age. As the years pass we forget how to play. But play is essential! It energizes us, increases optimism, eases burdens and provides joy. Now, thanks to the pioneering genius of our founder, Gabriel H. Penn, you can experience that joy again.

Actually experience it.

Just as you remember.

Devin stopped reading. He thought back to his meeting with the Administrator and the way she'd smiled when he mentioned the Visitors.

They weren't visiting the Home looking for kids to adopt, he thought, with a shock of understanding. They came to become kids again. Literally. To run and jump and throw and catch. To eat marshmallows around a campfire and swim in the pool and put a jigsaw puzzle together.

They came to play. And the kids were their toys.

Numbly he replaced the brochure on the pile, his eyes traveling across the room to the portrait on the far wall. He'd seen that face before. He'd seen it in his nightmare of the little boy. And he'd seen it in the window of his room. He'd thought a giant was peering in at him, but it was worse than that. It was his own reflection.

Devin stared down at the ring on his hand. An eagle, just like the one on the hood of the large sleek car . . .

I'm saving you for something special.

What could be more "special," Devin thought, than to swap bodies with the great Mr. Gabriel Penn himself?

But why me? Devin thought. Why swap with me?

Because he was different, he saw the world in a way that others didn't: richer, far more colorful, alive with sound and sensation. But there was more to it than that. It was also because of the farm. He'd been sheltered there, kept from knowledge of the outside world and all its fears. That made him different too. The Administrator had called him the most unusual child she had ever come across. Unusual enough to persuade her father to visit the Home at last and try out his own invention for himself.

She had used him as bait, he thought. A worm held dangling to catch a rare fish.

Devin didn't know how he made it back to his room without being discovered, because he made no effort to be careful. He shuffled along toward the stairs as fast as he could, his heart bursting with effort, shooting pains running up his back at each lurch of his hips. He knew he looked grotesque, Gabriel Penn with bare feet trying to run down a corridor and managing only a wheezing, panicky trot. But he was past caring what he looked like. He just wanted to get back to his room, curl up in the bed, and wait out the long hours until he was free again.

He reached his room at last. The minute he was inside he reached up and placed the hairpin on the tiny ledge of the doorframe. Then he sank down, exhausted.

Luke would figure it out, he thought. Luke and the others would know what to do.

Eighteen

THE TROUBLE WAS, LUKE didn't believe him. Malloy and Kit were no better.

"Sounds like just another dream," Malloy said. "A really bad one. Sometimes they do seem totally real . . ."

Kit nodded. "You just have to suck it up, Devin. I told you before."

"But it wasn't a dream," Devin cried. And he started explaining it all over again.

They were sitting in the small meadow. Devin had gathered them there because it was out of the way and he knew they wouldn't be overheard. He had spent the rest of his stay at the Place lying on his bed, pretending to sleep when Mrs. Babbage came in and out but fighting real sleep with all his might. He didn't want any more nightmares. He'd kept his gaze away from the window

and his reflection, counting the minutes, his mind struggling with the knowledge that as he lay there helpless,
Gabriel Penn had taken over his body and was using his
mouth to talk, his legs to run. There was a stranger in his
skin and the thought of it left Devin weak with outrage
and horror.

Finally, at the end of the second day in the Place, a
deep sleep came over him, too strong to fight. The shot
they'd given him was wearing off, and it was the sleep of
return. The minute he'd woken in his own bed, he had
run to find the others. But now they wouldn't listen.

"I saw the brochure!" he insisted. "They're selling this
place as a kind of treatment for old people . . . They're
selling us."

Luke frowned and rubbed his forehead. "It can't be
right, Devin. A couple of visits ago, they forgot to bring
me the drink. Doing without it for a whole morning
didn't make me remember anything. It just hurt like
hell."

"Maybe it's not just the drink," Devin argued.
"Maybe there's something in the shot that makes you
lose memory, and the drink just helps it along."

"Then why would it happen to me and not to you?"

Devin was tempted to say that his grandfather had
come back from the dead to help him, but he didn't
think it would be very convincing.

"I don't know, it just did."

"It happened when you smelled the soap," Kit said. She turned to the others. "His senses are different, remember? Everything is stronger for him. Maybe the smell was strong enough to break through." She turned to Devin. "Is rosemary special for you in any way?"

He thought of the grave at the top of the hill.

"Yes," he said. "Yes, it is."

"So they're swapping us with old people?" Malloy cried out incredulously.

Luke was silent. "I suppose it's possible," he said at last.

"No it's not!" Malloy burst out. "It's impossible times ten."

"Okay," Luke said, talking very fast. "I once did this Hi-Speed course on the biology of the brain. And in theory, it is possible—"

"You're telling me that people can go around swapping their bodies?"

"Not swapping bodies!" Luke snapped. "It's not that. It's swapping minds. I know that sounds like the same thing, but it's not. It's completely different."

"I don't get it," Malloy argued. "Why is swapping brains any different?"

Luke jumped up in agitation. "No! Not brains!" he cried. "I said minds!"

"But how do they do it?" Devin said. "How do they swap our minds?"

Luke sat down, but he kept on talking just as fast as before. Devin tried his best to follow, but it was hard. Luke seemed to be saying that Gabriel Penn—or a team of scientists working for him—could, in theory, have found a way to see all the connections that made up a person's mind and they could have developed a method—using a combination of biology, chemistry, and technology—to transfer one person's mind patterns into another person's brain, at least for a while.

"So you're saying it is possible," Malloy said slowly.

Luke nodded to himself, caught up in thought. "Amazing, really, completely amazing . . . and very cool."

"It's not cool!" Malloy half shouted. "It's terrible! It's . . . it's like stealing your soul."

"Yeah, that too," Luke said.

Devin glanced at Kit, but she had her head down and was tugging at the grass, pulling out clumps and flicking them away.

Things were starting to be clearer to Devin now.

The reason the Home was so old-fashioned wasn't just because the Visitors liked to remember the past, it was so they could actually experience the past. The group activities weren't for the children; they were only organized to provide extra play for the Visitors. Even the name of the Home itself now made sense. It wasn't a home for children but for childhood: the Visitors' childhoods.

It was obvious now why the kids became "spoiled."

Over time, it must be devastating to a child's mind to be treated like that. No wonder Pavel had been struck dumb and Jared had started behaving as if he were five years old.

"We act crazy when we're in the Dream," he said. "But it's not us, is it? It's the Visitors who are acting crazy."

"Yeah," Malloy agreed, looking as if he might be sick. "They probably can't believe how good it feels to be a kid again."

"But why do we have the dreams?" Devin asked. "Why do we have such bad dreams?"

"My guess is that they're leftovers," Luke said. "Really negative emotions can actually change the makeup of the brain itself. We're using their brains, remember? So the Visitors must leave bits of themselves behind—the bad bits."

Devin thought of the little boy in the dream with his terrible old man's face who had sobbed as if his heart would break. Who was he? And what had he done to become a leftover in Penn's brain?

"Now do you agree that we've got to escape?" Malloy cried. "We can't go to the Place again, not knowing this."

Luke nodded. "Bad as it was before, this makes it ten times worse."

Devin glanced again at Kit. She had gone pale but she was still plucking at the grass, taking no part in the discussion.

"Kit? What do you say?"

She gave him an odd, defiant look. "I don't know," she said, "I don't know. I have to think about it, okay?"

"What's to think about?" Malloy demanded. But Kit just shook her head and refused to answer.

✦ ✦ ✦

Devin found her later that day, down by the kennels. She had taken Frisker to visit the other puppies, and all four dogs were tumbling wildly, frantic with joy. Devin couldn't help smiling at the sight. Kit was smiling too, and it gave him hope that she'd come out of whatever strange mood she'd been in.

"You okay?"

She looked at him and then looked away.

"Sure," she said tightly. "Why wouldn't I be?"

"We'll get out of here," he said. "Don't worry. We'll figure out a way. Luke's smart, and so is Malloy in his own way. And you're tougher than anyone."

"What if I don't want to get out?"

Devin stared at her.

"I'm not going anywhere," she said.

"But they're using us! Kit, weren't you listening?"

"I can take it. Like you say, I'm tough. I'm staying until I get adopted."

"By . . . a Visitor?"

She shrugged.

"Why would you want to be adopted by the same

people who've been doing this terrible stuff?" Devin protested. "People who've used you like that could never really love you."

Kit jumped to her feet, her fists clenched. "Love! Who said anything about that? I've never been loved and I've gotten along just fine."

Devin wanted to tell her she was wrong about never being loved, but he couldn't find the words.

"Love!" she repeated in a scornful voice. "Listen, the people who'll adopt me will be old, very old. That means they'll die soon; and when parents die, their children inherit all their stuff."

"So it's about that," Devin said quietly, thinking of her dollhouse furniture and the way her face had looked as she imagined it being real and all hers. "It's just about having stuff."

"You don't understand!" she cried. "Of course it's about having stuff! Rich people don't get hurt, Devin. They don't get beaten. For the first time in my life I'll be safe."

She scooped Frisker into her arms, and before Devin could say anything, she hurried away, her shoulders hunched, her face buried in the puppy's soft fur.

Nineteen

THE RULE AMONG THE children was that nobody should look at anyone in the Dream. But over the next couple of days Devin made a point of watching them carefully. There were currently three: a boy named Corey, a tall girl with long, blond hair, whose name he didn't know, and Missie.

Now that he knew that there were Visitors' minds inside their bodies, their behavior, which had seemed so odd before, made perfect sense. He remembered his aching limbs back in the Place and tried to imagine what it would feel like to be old one minute and very young the next. It must be thrilling, he thought. It must be the best feeling in the world.

In the beginning, the children in the Dream could barely keep still. Missie turned cartwheels on the lawn, her skirt around her ears, her shoes tossed off. Corey ran from one attraction to the other, jumping on the trampoline and randomly kicking at things as if to test out the strength of his legs. The blond girl simply hopped from one foot to the other, apparently astonished at her own balance. They were like new lambs, he thought, or colts: giddy with energy, amazed at the working of their own arms and legs.

After this first stage of euphoria, they seemed to settle down a fraction. But they still moved in a state of wonder, as if their bodies were suits of fabulous clothes to be touched and admired.

All of them, without exception, spent a lot of time simply gazing around. But they didn't look at things the way that Devin had noticed children—real children— looked. Real children observed the world in an open, matter-of-fact sort of way. But the Visitors peered and stared, marveling like tourists in some new and incredible land.

They didn't play like real children, either. They were not intent and businesslike with their toys. Instead they seemed incredulous, examining each item as if they could barely believe their eyes. It was understandable, Devin thought. It had been decades, after all, since they had last held a building block or watched a model train chugging around a track or dressed a doll. He had never seen such toys himself before arriving at the Home, but he realized how familiar they must seem to the Visitors, as familiar as the nests in the barn and Glancer were to him.

In the dining room, they always heaped their plates up high. It puzzled Devin slightly, until he remembered the tiny, careful meals he'd been given during his visits to the Place when he'd been in the body of Gabriel Penn. After half a lifetime of eating balanced, healthy food, the Visitors couldn't get enough roast beef and bread and butter and chocolate cake. They ate for the joy of it without fear of weight gain, crumbling teeth, or getting enough vitamins.

Devin could understand it, but even so, their selfishness sickened him.

He glanced at Corey. The Visitor that had taken over his body had a sharp knife and was carelessly carving his initials into the wood of the dining room table. That knife could slip and cut the small hands that held it. But what did the Visitor care about that? There would be a moment of pain, but someone else would bear the scar forever.

Devin turned his head away, unable to watch any longer.

He thought of what Vanessa had said about how he had behaved when he was in the Dream. How he'd licked the grass and touched everything. It was Gabriel Penn who had done those things, carried away by the novelty of Devin's mixed-up senses. It made Devin feel small and almost worthless, as if he didn't really belong to himself any longer.

You have to keep your standards in a world where everything is slipping and sliding.

His grandfather was right. He was Devin. He belonged only to himself. And he would fight to keep it that way.

Devin pushed back his chair and went out into the courtyard.

The sunlight was almost blinding. According to Luke, it hadn't rained here for weeks and weeks. The longer the time between rainfalls, the fiercer the storm would be when it came. But there was no sign of it now. That wispy cloud he had seen days ago had disappeared.

A car pulled up in the driveway on the other side of the courtyard. Devin shaded his eyes, watching it. Then Roman appeared from one of the buildings with Megs trailing behind him. The door of the car opened and Roman got in. It reversed, turned, and started back down the driveway toward the main gates. For a little while Megs gave chase, her yellow bow bobbing wildly. Then she stood still, a forlorn little figure staring and waving as the car disappeared from view.

Roman must be off to the city to get more victims, Devin thought. He'd wondered whether the boy had turned traitor to avoid going to the Place, but now it occurred to him that there was nothing stopping Roman from simply staying in the city and never coming back.

Unless he was being paid.

He was doing it for the money, just like the Administrator. While the kids suffered, they were both happily raking in the cash.

◆ ◆ ◆

Devin needed to take his mind off things, if only for a short time. He went to the farmyard and stood watching the animals. Fulsome nosed his way over to him and nudged his leg. Devin rummaged in his pocket and found a piece of leftover cheese that he had saved for him.

"How many fingers am I holding up?" he asked the pig. But Fulsome just stood there, waiting patiently for his treat. Only Malloy could get him to do tricks. The boy had an understanding of animals that seemed almost magical. It was probably his Nomad upbringing, Devin thought. He liked the sound of Nomads. The way they lived didn't seem so different from his grandfather's ideas. Perhaps one day Malloy would take him to visit one of their camps.

Perhaps.

Devin tossed Fulsome the cheese and turned away. He wandered off toward the courtyard. Passing by the kennels, he heard voices. The Administrator and Mrs. Babbage. They were coming down the path in the opposite direction. Devin didn't think he could bear to see them. He ducked behind the kennel wall.

"He was told to come back tomorrow." That was the Administrator talking. Devin could only just make out the words.

Mrs. Babbage mumbled something in reply.

"He was told to find at least two," he heard the Administrator say. "Although I have serious doubts—"

They had stopped on the path. Devin shrank back against the wall, praying that they wouldn't look in his direction.

"I'm well aware of that, Babbage!" the Administrator snapped. Her voice lowered. Devin could hear only a phrase or two. She seemed to be talking about Visitors—new Visitors—and then there was a mention of "things being not up to standard." He kept as still as he could, listening.

"I won't have this sloppiness . . . certain individuals . . . no longer . . . I want it put right, a clean sweep . . ."

Mrs. Babbage murmured a question.

"Do try and keep up!" the Administrator snapped. "It's perfectly obvious! It's only because we've had such a shortage that I've tolerated it." Her voice lowered again. ". . . the teddy bear for one . . . wretched little fire . . . long overdue . . ."

"I thought you said she was not . . ." Mrs. Babbage's voice was plaintive.

"I don't care what I said!" the Administrator said, suddenly loud. "He makes no effort! He has not kept his side of the bargain, so I feel no obligation to keep mine."

Devin heard her heels clacking against the path as she strode away and then the softer, more rapid patter of Mrs. Babbage's shoes as she hurried to catch up.

He had the feeling that whatever it was they'd been talking about was important. He just wished he could have heard more. He might have if he'd had the courage to creep nearer. But he'd been too frightened of being discovered.

Kit would have made sure she heard the whole thing, he thought. At least the old Kit would have. The old Kit wasn't afraid of anything. But as he hurried back toward his room, he wondered whether this was true.

He was starting to think that he didn't know her as well as he'd thought he did.

Twenty

DEVIN WASN'T THE ONLY one who was wondering about Kit. He soon found out that Luke and Malloy had been watching her too. The two boys had told Devin to meet them in the small meadow. They wanted to talk about escape.

Devin waded through the long grass, threaded with wild flowers. The others were already there, Luke with a sheaf of papers in his hand, Malloy lying on his back and staring at the sky with a piece of grass in his mouth.

"Where's Kit?" Devin asked as he approached. Malloy sat up and glanced at Luke.

"We didn't ask her to come," Luke said, without looking up from his notes.

"Why not?"

Malloy grimaced. "One of Luke's theories. And I have to admit he's got a point."

"What?" Devin demanded.

"Sit down," Luke said. "Okay, this is kind of hard to talk about . . ."

"Awkward!" Malloy chimed in.

Luke gave him a look and Malloy fell silent.

"It's to do with that stuff we were talking about before," Luke explained. "You know, the bad dreams and how we thought they were leftovers from the Visitors. Bad stuff that had happened to them which had become part of their brain?"

Devin nodded. "I remember."

"It got me thinking," Luke continued. "When Roman first told you about the Home, back in the city, did he ask you about where you'd come from and if your home had been happy?"

Devin nodded again.

"He asked me too," Luke said. "Have you noticed how every kid in this place has come from a good home? Bad things might have happened to us, but we've all . . . we've all been loved. You, me, Malloy, Ansel and his dad. Karen had an aunt who looked after her, Missie was in a great family until her parents were killed in a car crash on the highway . . . My point is that we were all selected for that reason."

"But why?"

"So the Visitors won't be uncomfortable when they swap with us. Because we have no bad leftovers. Don't you get it? Being treated badly when you're a kid must do something to your brain, warp it in some way. Kit is the only one here who doesn't fit the pattern. Roman made a mistake with her; she wasn't meant to come along, was she?"

"I said I wouldn't come if she didn't." Devin felt his face grow hot. "But I don't know what you're saying. Are you saying Kit's brain is warped? Because if you are, you're wrong."

"I'm not saying that," Luke muttered, looking away. "It's just that we don't know her like you do. And Malloy and me have been thinking . . . wondering . . . if we can trust her."

"This is wrong!" Devin burst out. "It's wrong and . . . and unfair. Kit would never do anything to hurt us!"

"Are you sure? Really sure?"

Devin paused. He thought of Kit's desperation to be adopted, how she said she would do whatever it took. Did this include gaining favor with the Administrator by betraying her friends? He shook his head.

"I'm sure," he said. "I know her. I'm sure."

"Well, we're not," Luke said. "And we can't take the chance."

"I'm sorry, Strange Boy," Malloy said, looking unhappy. "Really sorry . . ."

A tense silence fell. "So are you in or are you out?" Luke said abruptly.

For a second, Devin considered walking away. But there was time to convince them that Kit could be trusted. He sat down stiffly, apart from the others.

"I'm in," he said. "What's the plan?"

✦ ✦ ✦

The first thing to decide was whether to tell the others in the Home about what was really going on in the Place. Devin and Malloy felt that it was only fair that they should know, but Luke pointed out that it might lead to unrest, which would put the Administrator and the staff on high alert. He thought their chances of escape would be better if they kept it to themselves for now. After a moment of thought, Devin agreed to this on the condition that when they did get out, they would take all the others too.

"We can't leave anyone here," he insisted. "Not even one."

"I see your point," Luke agreed, "but it's going to make it harder."

The talk turned to the laser posts, the control box, and the key.

In order to get a large number of children out of the Home, they would have to disarm the posts. To do this they would need three things: access to the control box, the key to unlock it, and whatever code was almost certainly needed to turn the posts off. There was a fourth requirement: enough time after the posts were disarmed to effect a mass escape. But since this would depend largely on luck, they decided to focus on the first three.

Only the first seemed doable. To gain access to the control box, they would have to get the Administrator to leave her office and stay out for as long as it took. They thought it might be possible with some sort of diversion, although it would have to be a major one.

The key was a different matter. It hung around the Administrator's neck, and she had never been seen without it.

"Could we simply attack her?" Malloy wondered. "Knock her out or something?"

"I suppose so," Luke said, "although it would be risky. She's probably got alarm buttons all over the office, and if we took one step toward her, she'd set them off. Besides . . ." He looked around at the others. "No offense, but none of us is exactly that strong."

Malloy punched him in the shoulder.

"Ow!"

"Strong enough for you?"

But even Malloy had to concede that they had a better chance of escape if they could get the key without having to attempt force.

That left the code. Luke was hoping that it was a long, complicated one because that meant that it was probably written down somewhere. But where? And how would they get the time to look? How many people knew it? The Administrator of course, and perhaps Mrs. Babbage . . .

Gabriel Penn must know it too, or know where it's kept, Devin thought. He invented this whole place, after all.

Penn had returned within a few days of his first visit, and there seemed no reason to think he wouldn't come back again very soon. Was there any way to find the code then? He kept the question to himself, partly because it seemed like a very slim possibility, but mostly because the thought of having to return to the Place terrified him.

I'm not strong enough, he thought; not brave enough either.

After a few more moments of talk, the boys got up and walked back to the courtyard. Apart from the diversion idea, it didn't seem as though they'd accomplished much, and the knowledge seemed to hang heavily on all of them. Luke was particularly depressed. He walked along, his mouth moving soundlessly as if in deep and frustrating conversation with himself.

Just before they got back, he stopped and turned to the others.

"Not a word to anyone, right?" He looked hard at Devin. "You promise?"

Devin paused, and then nodded.

In the common room, Vanessa was holding court on the sofa. She had news.

"Roman's back with a new kid. That's what I heard."

"Boy or girl?" someone asked.

"Boy," Vanessa said. "But very short," she added disdainfully. "He looks way younger than he is."

"Where is he now?"

Vanessa smiled knowingly. "Where do you think?"

The new boy was in the dining room, eating as if his life depended on it. Which in fact it probably did, Devin thought, staring at the wispy figure hunched over a plate of steak. He was tiny, with a delicate manner and very pale skin. He wasn't wearing the usual neat jeans and shirt that all the boys in the Home wore, but had apparently kept on the clothes that he came in: a suit, shirt, and large red bow tie.

The suit was slightly threadbare and a little too small—the boy's wrists showed at the ends of the sleeves. But the shirt collar was straight and the bow tie very bright, a singing shade like the wind in the grass. If you saw him from a distance or didn't pay too much attention, you might imagine that he wasn't a homeless street urchin at all, but a boy from a good home—perhaps even from The Meadows itself.

"Hi," Devin said, sitting down next to him. "I'm Devin, what's your name?"

The boy wiped his mouth carefully on his napkin. "Caspar John Friedrich Farrilly. Are seconds permitted here?"

"You can eat as much as you want. Did you come from the city?"

Caspar nodded. He looked down and brushed the front of his jacket.

"Don't you like the clothes they gave you?" Devin said.

"Oh, I'm not taking off my suit," Caspar said quickly. "I might not be able to get it back."

"Okay," Devin said a bit uncertainly.

"This suit is absolutely vital," Caspar continued in the same grown-up tone. "It's my Edge. Is that pie? We're allowed dessert, right?"

Devin nodded and Caspar made a beeline for the food table. His suit really was getting small for him, Devin thought. In addition to the too short sleeves, the seams were stretched at his shoulders.

Malloy had wandered up, and now, as Caspar returned with a heaped plate, he gave him his customary grin. "Eat much more and you're gonna be busting out of those pants. You might want to think about putting some elastic in the waist there."

"Oh, I have," Caspar said very seriously. "Believe me, I have. But it turns out elastic is hard to find in the city."

Malloy looked at Devin and raised his eyebrows.

"This suit's my Edge," Caspar explained. "You have to have an Edge, don't you? Some people are fast or strong or good at thieving or big enough to push other people out of the way. I don't have any of that. I just have this suit."

"I don't get it," Malloy said.

Caspar put down his fork. "What do I look like to you?" he asked.

"Kind of stuck up, if you must know," Malloy said.

"Malloy!" Devin said. "No, Caspar, you don't . . ." But Malloy's comment seemed to give Caspar satisfaction.

"Stuck up! Exactly. Here's how it works. I stand on the corner looking lost and a bit scared and I tell people that my chauffeur failed to pick me up and I need to get back to my home in The Meadows only my cash was stolen by some ruffian kid. And it works. Not always, but just enough. They pat me on the head, look worried, and give me money. Of course, you can't do it in the same place too many days in a row. You have to move around. But even when that doesn't work, the suit can usually help me get what food I need. People don't suspect a kid dressed like me could be hungry enough to steal."

"That's genius," Malloy said.

"Thank you," Caspar John Friedrich Farrilly said with great dignity. He tugged at his cuffs. "All the same, I'm glad to be here. You may have noticed that I am slightly on the short side, although my mom used to tell me it didn't matter. 'You're big inside,' she'd say. 'A big spirit is better than great height.' She never explained to me why I couldn't have spirit *and* height, and every single night, I prayed to grow. But lately I've been doing the opposite. I've been praying to stay small enough for this suit. Every night, I hang up the jacket so it won't crease, and hope I can still fit into it tomorrow." He looked down at the half-demolished pie on his plate as if seeing it for the first time. "I guess I won't need to do that anymore," he said slowly. "Now that I'm here, I guess I'm safe."

Devin and Malloy exchanged glances.

He'd find out soon enough what lay in store for him at the Home. Perhaps Devin could break it gently to him as he showed him around.

"You want a tour?" he asked.

"Definitely!" Caspar exclaimed. "This place looks incredible!"

✦ ✦ ✦

As it turned out, the tour ended much sooner than Devin anticipated—in the common room, after barely fifteen minutes.

"We sort of hang out in here," Devin said, waving his arm over the place. Caspar went over to look at the books. He pulled one halfway out and then looked up at the wall.

"What are all those pictures?" he said.

Devin hesitated. He understood now why Luke had been so reluctant to tell him about the Home when Devin first arrived. It felt almost cruel to destroy Caspar's happiness at being there.

The boy had replaced the book and was now peering at the photographs.

"Who are those people? And the kids—are they kids from here?"

Devin nodded unwillingly.

"I know him," Caspar said, pointing to one of the photos. His whole face had changed.

"Saw him just two days ago . . ." Caspar's voice was very low.

Devin looked at the picture. "You know Ansel?"

Caspar nodded.

"You saw him in the city? That must have been a while ago. Before he got here."

"No, I told you," Caspar muttered. "I saw him two days ago."

"You can't have," Devin said. "Ansel was adopted from here over a week ago. He went to live with the ladies in the picture. He went to be their son. You must have met someone who looked like him, that's all."

Caspar shook his head. "No. It was him. I'll never forget that face. Not as long as I live."

Devin looked around to make sure they weren't being overheard. A couple of the younger children had entered the common room and were starting a jigsaw puzzle. "Let's go to my room," he said. "You can tell me about it there."

According to Caspar, he had seen Ansel, or a boy who looked very much like him, in the old school gym in the city where the children went when it rained. Although it hadn't rained in weeks near the Home, Caspar had been pleased about this big storm in the City, because it had given him a chance to wash his shirt.

"I have a secret place where I hang it up," he explained. "You have to keep your shirt white, or your suit doesn't look as good. I get the shirt wet in the rain and then it dries again and it's clean."

But Caspar didn't like being in the school gym, partly because he was frightened of some of the other, larger boys and partly because his suit jacket scratched against his bare skin and he was worried—as always—that while he was away, someone would find his shirt and take it. He sat in the darkest corner, with his knees pulled in to his chest, watching and waiting for the rain to be over.

He knew most of the other kids by sight, particularly a gang of four older boys who were occupying a space right in the middle of the gym, staring threateningly at the other kids and shoving those who got near. But one boy in the gym was new to Caspar, and he watched him carefully. The boy was big and good-looking, but he seemed dazed. He sat with a blank look on his face, hugging a backpack to his chest as though it contained something very valuable. He didn't seem to know that in the city if you had something valuable, you kept it hidden. Nor did he seem to know that he had attracted the attention of the gang. He just sat there in a dream.

"He didn't have an Edge," Caspar said. "No Edge at all."

Caspar had felt bad for the boy, but by the morning, he'd forgotten him. The sun was out again and he needed to see if his shirt was still where he'd left it. He was planning to start telling his story about the chauffeur and the stolen cash in a different part of the city. It was time he found a new place. People were beginning to look at him very suspiciously, and just the day before, he'd been chased down the street by a man who'd given him money in the past and realized he'd been tricked.

The shirt was where he had left it and it was already dry. Caspar breathed a sigh of relief, put it on carefully, and set out.

He was crossing a small parking lot surrounded by abandoned buildings when he saw the boy again. The gang was surrounding him, trying to get his bag. Caspar immediately ducked into the shadow of a wall. One of the gang shoved the boy hard in the shoulder, almost knocking him down, another swung a fist into his face, a third snatched at the bag, yanking on the straps. Caspar wondered why the boy didn't just give it up. But he

222

wouldn't. He clutched the bag against his chest as if it was more than merely valuable, as if it was part of his body itself.

Caspar heard a yell of triumph. They had the boy on the ground now and had tugged the bag free. The biggest gang member opened it and looked inside. Then he flung it down again with a howl. Whatever he'd been expecting, food or money, clearly wasn't there.

It seemed to drive the gang into a fury. Caspar shrank back against the wall, his heart pounding and his hands sweaty. They were laying into the boy now, powered by disappointment and rage. The boy was still on the ground, his hands over his head, his body curled up.

"What did you do?" Devin asked. Caspar hung his head.

"Nothing," he whispered.

He'd squeezed his eyes shut and put his hands over his ears, trembling in the shadow of the wall. After a long time, he looked again. The gang was gone. The boy lay on the ground without moving, his backpack by his side. Caspar crept toward him. There was blood on the boy's head, and his eyes were closed. Caspar put his hands under the boy's shoulders and dragged him inch by inch into one of the nearby buildings. It was cooler in there, the light filtered through windows thick with dust.

He hesitated, then took off his jacket, bunched it into a pillow and slid it under the boy's head.

"He bled on it. But luckily only on the inside." He opened his jacket and Devin saw the huge stain, dark against the gray silk lining.

Caspar gave the boy water, although he didn't drink much. Then he carefully washed the boy's face and sat down beside him. He sat with him all afternoon. In the early evening, just as the light was starting to soften, the boy died.

"I don't think he was in pain," Caspar said. "He didn't look like he was in pain. I went out and got his backpack. You'll never guess what was inside."

Devin was silent.

"A soccer ball," Caspar said. "All that for just a plain old soccer ball."

Twenty-One

"I'm not listening to you!" Kit half-shouted. She shoved her hands over her ears. "Go away, I'm not listening!"

"You have to listen," Devin said. They were in Kit's room. He had gone to find her as soon as he could. Frisker was curled up in a ball on the bed. When Kit started shouting, he leaped up and began to bark, his yelps tiny and squeaking.

"You have to listen," Devin said again. "Ansel is dead. He never was adopted. There is no adoption. We stay here until we're all useless, Spoiled, whatever you want to call it, and then they dump us back into the city and they don't care whether we live or die."

"It's a lie. That new kid is just causing trouble. Or maybe he did see someone who looked like Ansel.

Or maybe Ansel has a brother. The real Ansel's been adopted." She stared at Devin almost pleadingly. "You saw his photo. That's the proof."

Devin didn't reply. He reached into his pocket and took out the picture, smoothing the creases. "I took it from the wall," he said quietly. "Something always bugged me about this picture and now I know what it is. Do you remember the campout? How Ansel caught Frisker? He fell on his face and had a big scrape on his cheek. You wiped it yourself."

Devin held the picture out for her to see. "Look at his face. There's not a mark on him. They faked the photo. They faked all the photos on that wall. They did it to keep us quiet and well behaved."

Kit's face went as red as if Devin had slapped her. Then all the blood drained from her cheeks and the whole upper part of her body seemed to cave in on itself. She sank to the floor.

"I knew it," she wailed. "I knew, I knew. All along, right from the start. The minute I got here I thought, this place stinks worse than the leather of my dad's old belt."

She was crying now, her face blurred and twisted.

"I didn't know what was wrong," she sobbed, "but I could feel it. I just didn't want to think about it. I wanted Frisker and good food and nice clothes and . . . and I wanted to be adopted. The more you tried to talk to me, the angrier I got because you were spoiling it, Devin. But I knew you were right. Deep down I knew it."

"It's okay," Devin said helplessly. She had stopped crying, but there was still despair on her face. He sat down on the floor beside her. "It's okay," he repeated.

"No," she said, "no it's not. I lied to myself. I thought I was tough, but that's only on the outside. Inside, I'm nothing. The Administrator was right, Devin. There's something wrong with me. I'm damaged."

Devin thought about her, the whole of her. Her fierce, freckled face, the way she ran and climbed and looked toward the sky, her skilled thievery and love of beauty, her sparkling rooftop and the scars upon her back. All her daring and her passion and her weakness and her sorrow.

"You're not damaged," he said. "You're perfect."

Kit buried her head in her hands and burst into tears again.

"Don't cry," Devin begged. "It's going to be okay." He knew he had promised to stay silent, but he couldn't help himself. "We're planning to get out, to get everyone out. It's not just talk anymore. We haven't gotten very far with the plan yet, but we will." And he told her all about the diversion, and their idea of possibly attacking the Administrator to get the key, and the difficulty with the code.

"I've got an idea about how to do it. It might work . . ."

Kit's head was still buried in her hands, but she had stopped crying. And Devin could tell she was listening, because she had gone completely still.

◆ ◆ ◆

Of the three boys, Luke seemed the most devastated by Devin's news. Malloy cried when he heard about Ansel and crept off silently to mourn on his own. But he had never wanted to be adopted and wasn't too surprised to find out it had all been a hoax. Luke, on the other hand, seemed to turn in on himself; his face grew tighter and his twitching worsened. He became morose and then downright mean.

They were still talking about Caspar's story next day in the dining room, although they were careful to avoid being overheard.

"You haven't told anyone else, have you?" Devin asked. "I don't know what would happen if everyone knew."

Malloy shook his head.

"No one. Although I think Roman might have a clue. Luke and I were crossing the courtyard yesterday and talking about it and I turned around and there he was. He might have overheard.

"Rotten sneak," he added.

"He doesn't matter," Luke muttered. "Nobody talks to him except for Megs, and she probably wouldn't pay any attention. Too busy trying to set fires."

"Sooner or later, someone's gonna hear, though. Like

228

Vanessa," Malloy said. "Once she knows, there's no stopping it. The good news is that I've got a great idea for a diversion."

Malloy's idea unsurprisingly involved his friend Fulsome. According to Malloy, the pig was virtually psychic and the two of them could communicate without words. Besides, he said, the diversion would be a chance for Fulsome to redeem himself after the fiasco in the courtyard.

Luke listened to him chatter on without saying anything.

"He nearly saved us last time," Malloy said, "only I didn't give him complete instructions."

Luke suddenly banged his fist hard on the table. "Are you a moron? Are you a complete idiot?"

Malloy looked astonished. Luke had always been sarcastic with him, but never unkind.

"I can't believe you're even thinking of using that stupid pig again," Luke cried. "This isn't a game, Malloy. This isn't another one of your jokes. Ansel died. Don't you get it? He died."

Luke pushed away from the table and strode out of the room, his whole body jerking as he went. Malloy's mouth was open.

"It will work," he said sadly, "I mean it will probably . . . I thought he trusted me . . ."

"I'll go and talk to him," Devin said.

Luke didn't answer when he knocked on the door of his room. When Devin pushed it open, papers swirled and rustled around his feet. The floor was covered with Luke's notes and calculations. He had obviously shoved them all off his desk, along with the photograph of his parents. Devin spotted it lying half under the bed. There was a crack in the glass over the picture.

Luke was sitting at the empty desk, his head sunken into his shoulders.

"What do you want?" he muttered without looking up.

"Are you okay?"

"Oh, great. Never been better."

"Why'd you throw everything onto the floor?"

"Because it's trash."

"It's all your work," Devin protested. He knelt and started to gather up the papers.

Luke was biting his bottom lip so hard that Devin thought he might draw blood.

"It's trash," he repeated. "Like our escape plan. Malloy says himself that he's a chicken. That's who's going to get us out of here? A chicken and a pig? I'm never getting out."

"You have to," Devin said. He picked up the photograph with the cracked glass and placed it carefully on the desk. "You have to so you can bust your parents out of jail, remember?"

Luke made a sound that was meant to be a laugh but sounded more like a rattle.

"My dad! I've been thinking a lot about him. He stole more money than he could possibly spend in ten fabulous lifetimes. But he wouldn't stop. He just kept going and going. He told me that greed makes idiots out of people. Well, that makes him the biggest idiot in the world, doesn't it? Except that he's not. I'm the biggest idiot in the world."

"Why would you say that? How can you think that?"

"I should have seen it!" Luke cried. "I should have figured out what was going on here. If I had, I might have saved Ansel. He was a good kid. He didn't deserve what happened to him . . . But they tricked me, they made an idiot out of me, and I'm supposed to be some kind of genius?"

"You are a genius," Devin said simply. "You're the smartest person I've ever met."

"Yeah? And how many people have you met, Farm Boy? It must be all of ninety-three."

Luke slumped, his head and shoulders on the desk, his long hair covering his face.

"We'll work it out," Devin said, his words tumbling out with anxiety. "You really are a genius, and Malloy's a kind of genius too with animals, and now that Kit understands we have to get out, she'll help. She's amazing, you know, she's—"

"You told Kit?" Luke had raised his head and was staring at him. "You told Kit about the escape?"

Devin fell silent.

"That's great. Just great. You promised not to tell her, but you did."

"I know," Devin said. "I broke my promise. I'm sorry."

"A lot of good that does. The damage is done. Where is Kit, by the way? I haven't seen her all day."

Now that Devin thought about it, neither had he. The last time he'd seen her was the night before, in the dining room. She had sat by herself in a corner, picking at her food. Since then there had been no sign of her at breakfast or at lunch.

"I haven't seen her either," he admitted.

"So let me get this straight," Luke said. "You run off and tell Kit all about how we're going to create a diversion, possibly attack the Administrator, try to disarm the posts, and get everyone out, and then Kit mysteriously disappears for hours and hours. I'm not liking the sound of this, Devin. I'm not liking it at all."

But Devin had stopped listening. He was looking out the window to the courtyard below. The door to the tower had opened and Kit had come out. She was walking right toward their rooms and there were two security guards, one on either side, walking along with her.

"Oh, no," whispered Luke. "They're coming this way."

Twenty-Two

THEY HEARD THE ENTRANCE door below bang open and then heavy steps on the stairs. Luke grabbed Devin's arm. "Don't say anything, not a word. I'll tell them it was all my doing, that I influenced you, forced you into it . . ."

The steps came down the corridor toward Luke's room and passed by. Devin ran to the door and listened. "They're going down to the end of the hall. They're going to Kit's room."

There was a rattle of keys, the sound of the footsteps coming back and down the stairs again. Devin flung open the door and ran to Kit's room.

"Let me in!"

"They've locked the door," came her voice. "Hang on a sec."

He heard a scratching at the keyhole and the door opened.

"That lock is pathetic," Kit said. "A cross-eyed sloth could pick it."

"With one arm tied behind its back," she added. She looked at Devin and Luke.

"What are you staring at? Are you going to come in or not?"

"Where've you been?" Devin asked. She closed the door behind him and dragged a chair over, wedging the top of it under the door handle. "Just to be on the safe side," she said.

"Where did you go?" Devin asked again.

"For a long time, nowhere. I was too nervous to eat breakfast and I sat here for a couple of hours kind of psyching myself up."

"For what?" Luke demanded.

"I'll tell you if you let me just talk, okay?"

She had sat on her bed for a long time, Kit told them. She was thinking through everything she had to do. At last she was ready. She got what she needed from the drawer in her dresser and slipped on a dress with deep pockets. Then she took a deep breath and went out looking for Mrs. Babbage.

After a long search, Kit found her in the laundry room, counting towels.

"I need to see the Administrator," Kit said. "It's very important."

A look of annoyance flickered over Mrs. Babbage's face, quickly replaced by a smile.

"What's it about, Kit, dear?"

"I can't tell you."

"The Administrator is ever so busy," Mrs. Babbage said. "She can't be disturbed. You don't want to get into trouble do you?"

"You're the one who'll get in trouble if you don't let me see her," Kit said. "Believe me."

Mrs. Babbage hesitated, her eyes narrowing.

"All right," she said at last. "I'll let her know you're coming. But I do hope, Kit, dear, that it is important. I'd hate to see you punished, you know."

Kit didn't bother replying. She went at once to the tower.

The Administrator was sitting behind her desk, her hair shining as if it had been polished strand by strand. Kit made a note of what she was wearing: an icy pink shirt with the top three buttons undone. She stepped forward.

"You said it was important," the Administrator stated.

"Yes." Kit glanced over to the small birdcage. The cover was off, and she could see Darwin on his perch.

He was wiping his beak against the bars of the cage, over and over, making a rasping, clacking noise. The Administrator didn't seem to notice the sound. Perhaps it had been going on for so long that she had simply gotten used to it. Kit felt a stab of pity for the bird, and then shook it off. Pity made you weak, she thought. She had to be strong.

"I'm waiting," the Administrator said. Kit walked forward until she was almost at the desk.

"It is important. Important to me," she said in a rush. "It's about getting adopted." She put her hands on the desk and leaned forward. "I really want to get adopted, I mean I really want to and . . . and I want to tell you that I'll do whatever it takes to get to the top of the list."

The Administrator stared at her. Kit leaned even further forward. Her hands moved fast, but not as fast as they could, she made sure of that.

"This is not what I would call—" the Administrator began. Then her eyes widened. "Open your hand!" she snapped. "I saw you. Open it now!"

Kit appeared to tremble slightly. She took a step back and hung her head. Slowly she uncurled her fist. In her palm were four blue marbles from the bowl on the Administrator's desk. The Administrator pushed back her chair and strode around to the front of the desk.

"You dared to come in here and disturb me so you could steal from me?" she said in a low voice.

Kit made a wailing noise and pitched forward. "I'm sorry!" she cried, clutching at the Administrator, "I'm sorry! They're so pretty and I . . . I can't help myself . . ."

The Administrator stiffened in disgust as Kit's arms went around her in a hug. The Administrator's arms shot up, jerky as a robot, and Kit heard her gasp. For a split second they stayed like that and then Kit let go and fell back. "I'm sorry," she said again and began to cry.

The Administrator brushed herself off with both hands. "You will go to your room," she said. "You will not come out. You will not eat. You will stay there until further notice."

"Yes, yes, I deserve that," Kit mumbled, wiping her eyes.

The Administrator was still frantically brushing at herself as if she could wipe away even the memory of having been touched.

"Oh," Kit cried. "You dropped something, your necklace. Under the desk there. I'll get it!" And without waiting for a reply she dropped to her hands and knees and groped under the desk. "Here it is," she said, handing it back. The Administrator took it without a word, her eyes fixed furiously on Kit's face. Two security guards had appeared.

"Take her to her room," the Administrator ordered the guards. "And make sure you lock the door."

✦ ✦ ✦

Devin and Luke stared at Kit. Her eyes were shining with triumph. She rummaged in the pocket of her dress and pulled something out. It was a little silver key.

"Remember my rule, Devin? Steal small and steal big? The Administrator was so busy thinking about me taking the stupid marbles that she didn't notice that I got this!"

"But what about when she sees it's gone?" Devin exclaimed. "She's bound to . . ."

Kit smiled. "I noticed that key and that chain around her neck the first time I met her. I saw that the chain was thin but the clasp was quite big. I notice things like that. I also noticed that the key looks a lot like one of the keys I brought with me from the city—from my special collection. When I grabbed her I undid the chain and threw it under the desk. Then I pretended to find it, and while I was under the desk, I swapped her key with mine. She won't notice the difference. People don't really look at their keys, do they? Not till they have to use them."

There was a stunned silence and then Luke stepped forward.

"I doubted you," he said simply. "I shouldn't have and I'm sorry."

"'S okay," Kit said, sounding very embarrassed but also very pleased.

Luke took the key and examined it carefully.

"You're right that people don't look at keys, but she

might. So we don't have much time. If we're going to do this, we have to do it soon."

"What do you mean, 'if'?" Kit demanded. "We've got everything we need except the code." She looked at Devin. "You had an idea about that, didn't you?"

"Kind of," Devin said hesitantly. "You see, they don't know that I've figured out what they're doing and they don't know I can move around the place. Maybe the code is somewhere in there and maybe I can find it."

"It's a big maybe," Luke said skeptically, "but I guess it's the best plan we've got."

"Only problem is," Kit said, "Devin's got to go to the Place again before we get out."

They were all silent. "It's okay," Devin said at last. "Don't worry. I'll be okay."

◆ ◆ ◆

Devin spent most of the next day wandering around aimlessly. He'd spoken bravely the day before, but he didn't feel brave. There was an ache in his throat, and his hands were sweaty, no matter how many times he wiped them on the front of his shirt.

The sky was just as blue as always, but the color had hardened as though covered by a thin film of burning ice. When Devin stared up, it seemed to glitter slightly, sending out a thin whine, as faint and insistent as a mosquito. He had heard this sound before. It was the noise of the sky being stretched tighter and tighter, like skin over clenched knuckles. They should have had a storm days ago, he thought. Instead it had just grown hotter.

Devin felt stretched too, pulled tight between desperate hope and terrible fear. He wanted more than anything to be sent to the Place again, but he also dreaded it with all his heart. He walked slowly up to the top of the hill where he had found the four-leaf clovers with Roman. The tower was on his right, just below him. To his left lay the maze and carousel. As usual, there was nobody riding the golden horses. Their manes flew back, and their eyes were wild, but they were trapped, speared through the heart by rigid poles, forced to turn in the same tight circle forever.

The mirrors at the top of the carousel flashed as they caught the sun and made the same noise as the sky, only louder. On the farthest edge of the horizon, where it met the line of trees at the perimeter of the Home, there was a blurring in the air as if someone had smudged it with the tip of a finger. Devin felt the muffled drumbeat of a headache against his skull.

Above the tower, the birds wheeled and scattered. There was something different about their flight and a new urgency to their shrieking. Birds had knowledge, he thought. They could feel the disturbance in the atmosphere. The strange heat, the tight, unbreakable sky.

Devin sat down in the long grass, watching them. He could sense disturbance in the weather too, just like the birds. He'd always assumed everyone had this ability, but he'd also thought everyone could see colors and sounds in the same way that he did. Kit had told him otherwise. A "power" she'd called it. A secret power.

Was it possible to have a power without realizing it?

Devin turned and lay on his stomach and rested his throbbing head in his hands. For most of his life there had been only his grandfather to explain things to him. What other powers might he have that he didn't even know about?

A breeze ruffled the grasses in the meadow. It was a feeble thing, almost spent already. From the other side of the grounds, the notes of the ice-cream truck tinkled faintly, half lost in the heat.

In a little while they would be laying out supper in the dining room. And then it would be night and another day gone. Devin didn't know how much more waiting he could take. What if Gabriel Penn never switched with him again? Maybe he was tired of it. Maybe he was dead. Old people did die suddenly sometimes. Devin rested his cheek against the ground and thought of his grandfather lying on the porch of the farmhouse, his big empty hands, his open eyes . . .

He felt a vibration in the earth, distant at first but growing stronger. Devin raised his head. Someone was toiling slowly up the hill toward him, head down.

It was Karen.

He waited until she was right in front of him, panting in the heat.

"It's okay," he said. "You don't have to say it." He got to his feet and brushed himself off.

Karen hung her head. "I'm sorry," she whispered, "I'm sorry, so sorry . . ."

"Don't be," Devin said. And he meant it. The hammering in his head was stronger than ever. He took a deep breath and set off walking toward the Place.

Twenty-Three

He was in the room at the top of the Place again. He opened his eyes and knew it instantly. He didn't need the rosemary soap this time to identify his location or remember who he was. The memory of the scent had wedged itself too tightly in his mind to be easily dislodged. All the same, he knew he couldn't afford to take the drugs that Mrs. Babbage would bring.

When she entered with the glass of liquid, he waited until she had gone and then got up and poured it down the sink. He had to do this as fast as he could because the temptation to drink it was very strong. Being inside somebody else's body felt worse than ever. Before, he'd been numbed a little by shock, but now the full horror of the situation washed over him. He longed to grab at his own flesh and tear it away as if it were some repulsive animal that had latched on to him and wouldn't let go. Yet, at the same time, he couldn't bear to touch himself. He stood shaking, nausea rising in his throat, his breath ragged with panic.

The code, he thought. The code.

In a little while he felt calmer. He went to the door and reached up for the hairpin on the ledge, his fingers groping through a thin layer of dust. For a second he thought it was gone, but then his fingers brushed against it and he heard himself wheeze with relief.

Devin didn't know where he should start looking for the code. He lurched slowly down the stairs, clinging to the rail with both hands. He'd seen offices on his last visit to the Place; perhaps he should begin there. At the bottom of the stairs, he turned left and shuffled into the first empty room he came to.

On the desk was a large screen. The moment he saw it, Devin felt a fresh clutch of panic. If the code was anywhere, it was surely in here, but he had no idea how the things worked. Why hadn't he thought of this before? He didn't even know how to turn it on. He stared at it. The screen was as thin as a piece of paper, and there were no buttons anywhere. He brushed his hand across the glass, and then tapped it a couple of times.

Nothing.

He walked around the desk to look at the back of the thing, feeling stupid and helpless. It was completely blank.

Perhaps he should go to the room with the brochures and the portrait of Gabriel Penn. Perhaps there was something there that might help. He crept down the corridor, not sure exactly where the room was. He'd ducked into it so quickly before . . . He looked into one room and then another, eventually finding it more from luck than anything else. It was the same as before except that the roses were red this time instead of yellow. Devin looked around, not knowing what to do next.

There was a low dresser with a number of drawers, and he was just about to go and have a look at it when he heard the sound of footsteps and then the Administrator's voice, loud in the corridor outside.

"If you'd like to follow me, please!"

The footsteps grew louder.

"This is our meeting room . . ."

Devin stood paralyzed. He had to hide. But where? If he'd been himself, if he'd been a boy, he would have simply dropped to his knees and crawled behind one of the huge chairs. But Gabriel Penn's old body simply couldn't bend fast enough. He'd be caught before he got halfway to the floor. He looked around wildly, saw a tall screen with a pattern of dragons and flowers on it, and staggered behind it, ducking his head only a second before the door to the meeting room opened.

"Please make yourselves comfortable," he heard the Administrator say. How different her voice sounded! It was almost soft. There was a sound of murmuring and shuffling and sighing and the plumping of cushions and gasps of relief as several people settled themselves into the chairs. The screen had three separate panels, joined together with hinges. Devin put his eye to the gap between two panels and peered through. The room was filled with six or seven Visitors, all seated. He could see the Administrator. She had a bundle of brochures and was handing them out, one by one. A staff member was busy serving drinks.

"I'll have water," he heard one woman say in a thin, querulous voice. "With bubbles. But it has to be the right kind of bubbles. Small bubbles. I must insist on the kind with the small bubbles."

"Scotch and soda for me," a man croaked. "Only hold the soda—heh-heh-heh."

"Perhaps we should begin," the Administrator said.

Through the gap in the screen, Devin watched her flat, black eyes as they ranged over the room.

"You have seen our facilities, the operations room, and the accommodation. And I've run through the process of what we offer here. If you have further questions, now is your opportunity to ask them."

"I want to know how much the whole damn thing costs!" It was the man who'd ordered the scotch and soda. "It can't be cheap."

"It isn't," the Administrator said without hesitation.

Then she named a sum so high that Devin wondered if he'd heard correctly.

The man gave a long whistle.

"Please consider what's involved," the Administrator continued smoothly. "And consider that this is a unique opportunity. We are the only place in the world to offer this service. The technology exists nowhere else but in this building. And after experiencing our Re-Play Treatment, one hundred percent of our clients agree that it was worth every penny of the cost. Their lives are, quite simply, transformed."

"But isn't it . . . I mean . . . isn't it . . . against the law?" Devin couldn't see who had spoken. The voice was low and rather timid. But he saw the Administrator smile.

"Technically, yes, it is," she agreed. "But the money you pay includes a fee that frees you from any legal responsibility whatsoever. Besides, I'm sure you'll agree that such trivial laws hardly apply to people such as yourself."

The Visitors exchanged glances and small, knowing smiles.

"Let me also take this opportunity," the Administrator continued, "to reassure you that the children at our Home are all in the best of health and couldn't be happier to be part of the program. They've told me on many occasions that they actually look forward to being of help to you. They consider it a great privilege."

Behind the screen, Devin clenched his fists tight. The room was filled with happy chatter.

The Administrator let them talk for a while and then clapped her hands. "If nobody has any more questions, I'd like to direct you to my office for further refreshments and the signing of contracts . . ."

With a seemingly endless amount of shuffling and sighing and heaving of limbs out of chairs, the whole group rose to their feet and exited the room. For a moment after they'd gone, Devin could hardly move from sheer rage. How easily the Visitors had accepted the Administrator's lies!

It's because they don't care, he thought. They just don't care about us.

But Devin couldn't afford to waste time with anger. It was late in the day and he was no nearer to finding the code than he had been before. And with the Place milling with Visitors, the chances of being caught were higher than ever. With a sinking heart, he decided to return to his room.

✦ ✦ ✦

Devin sat on the edge of his bed, too tired and anxious to shudder any longer at the sight of his bony knees and shriveled legs.

He hadn't been able to find the code. He'd failed.

He sat without moving for a long while. It grew dark outside. There was a quiet click as the lights in the room came on automatically. Devin raised his head. He was directly opposite the window, and in the glass he saw his reflection again. The face of a stranger. The face of Gabriel Penn.

He stood up and slowly stepped forward, forcing himself to look and not turn away. Gabriel Penn had once been handsome, and there was still a shadow of something fine and strong in the sharp lines of his cheekbones and the set of his broad forehead. But time had all but destroyed whatever attractiveness he might have had—time and a thousand heartless choices that had put money before kindness and ambition before love. It was a hard, shut-off face without a trace of kindness or feeling. Devin remembered Penn's first arrival at the Home, how he'd left the Administrator standing there without even bothering to get out of the car to greet her. Even his own daughter meant nothing to him.

But as Devin watched, something seemed to tremble behind Penn's cold eyes. Was it just a trick of the reflected light? Devin walked forward until he was close enough to the glass to put two hands up against it. He stared, searching.

There it was again, behind the eyes: the faintest flicker of heartache, a yearning for something—or someone— that was long gone and never to return. It was as feeble as a flickering candle, but it brought a gleam of humanity to Penn's face, like a light at the end of a long, dark tunnel.

Or maybe, Devin thought, he had it the wrong way around. Maybe it was a light at the start of the tunnel. All the way back to where Gabriel Penn had begun. And suddenly he knew who the boy was in the dream.

He had to find him again. He had to sleep.

He turned away and drew back the white sheets of the bed and lay down. He was frightened, but strangely calm. He closed his eyes.

There was no empty plain this time. Instead he dreamed of the farm, and it was more beautiful than it had ever been. It was morning and spring, the fields new green and the stream running fast and the air full of dandelion spores drifting on the breeze. Devin clattered down the steps of the porch and ran across the yard, looking for the little boy. He wasn't in the barn or the orchard. Devin ran around the side of the farmhouse.

He found him sitting on the stone wall, his small legs dangling. No old man's face this time, but the soft skin and wide blue eyes of a five-year-old child. He had a dandelion in his hand and was blowing on it, his little cheeks puffed out.

"You're him," Devin said. "When he was little. You're Gabriel."

The boy stared at him and then smiled. "It's not Gabriel, it's Gabe."

"You're in his head . . ."

"I'm part of him," the boy said.

"So you know . . . you know things about him." Devin said. "I need your help, Gabe."

"Are you lonely like me?"

Devin shook his head. A wind was picking up. The trees on the top of the hill swayed, and the long grass bent and sighed. "Do you know where the code is?" he asked. "Do you know how I can find it?"

"Is this a game?"

"Yes," Devin said. "A game . . ."

"Only I never get to play anymore. Not even ever. He grew up and left me behind."

"Please tell me. It's important."

The boy laughed, his face lit up with merriment. "But it's so easy! An easy game! It's not a mirror, silly!"

"I don't understand."

"You just stand and wave!" the boy cried. "And then you use the ball!"

The wind was even stronger now. It whistled through the stones in the wall and whipped the hair around Devin's face.

"What do you mean?"

But the boy bowed his head and twisted his hands in his lap.

"I miss him," he whispered. "I miss him bad."

"He misses you too, Gabe."

And with the strange insight that sometimes comes in dreams, Devin knew he spoke the truth. Gabriel Penn had lost all touch with the child he used to be. But he longed for him. Perhaps his childhood was the only time in his life that he'd ever been happy. He'd invented a way to swap minds so that people could feel like kids again, but it hadn't been enough for him. He must have known that it wouldn't get him any closer to the boy he once was because he'd never tried it for himself until now. Perhaps old age had made him desperate.

"But no matter how many times he swaps with me, it's not going to work," Devin said. "He'll never find you. He's done too many . . . terrible things."

"Then I'm lost," the boy said. "Where can I go? Can I stay here?"

"This is my farm." Devin said. "You don't belong here. You're a part of him."

"But now I'm a part of you too, aren't I?"

The idea should have been disturbing, but it wasn't.

He's innocent, Devin thought. Just an innocent little boy.

The wind had dropped and the meadow was starry with wildflowers. Blossoms drifted in the shady orchard. Down at the stream, the water ran clean and tawny, turning paddling feet to gold. There would come a day when a basket of apples would be dropped in the yard, and a grave dug amid the rosemary. But that was not today and today would last forever.

"Okay Gabe," Devin said, very gently. "You can stay here."

✦ ✦ ✦

It was morning when Devin woke. He lay very still for a moment or two, thinking. Most dreams, he thought, were perfectly clear when he was dreaming them. It was only when he woke up that they got muddled and confused. But this one was different. This one had made no sense while he was asleep. But now it did. Realization rushed over him. He heaved himself up.

It was hard to wait until he could get out of the room again. It seemed to him that Mrs. Babbage was being particularly slow when she came with his drink and breakfast. She took a long time arranging everything on the table, then came over to the chair where he was pretending to sleep and peered at him, her face very close.

"Nothing to say for yourself? Going to sleep all day are you?"

But at last she was gone and the corridor outside was quiet. Devin made for the stairs, his bones creaking and groaning. He didn't waste any time going into offices, but headed straight for the metal door he'd seen on his previous visit to the Place.

It's not a mirror, silly!

Devin stood in front of it. The metal was smooth and looked massively thick. There was no handle on the door and no buttons on the wall beside it.

You just stand and wave!

Devin raised his right hand, palm out and rested it against the frame of the door. He felt a soft vibration as invisible sensors briefly scanned his skin. A green light flickered above the door, then the metal slid back. Devin stepped inside.

It was a large room, completely empty apart from a huge table in the center with a top made of black glass. He shuffled forward uncertainly, and as he did, colors appeared on the surface of the table. Devin gaped in astonishment. A model of the Home had risen before his eyes, although it wasn't made of anything but light. Devin could see right through it. There were the court-yard and the tower, the outlying meadows, the farmyard, maze, and recreation building, all perfectly propor-tioned, floating in the air.

And there were the twelve laser posts arranged like the numbers on a clock.

Devin hobbled nearer, his heart pattering, missing a beat or two and then fumbling on again.

Stay alive, Gabriel Penn! Devin thought. Stay alive just long enough!

The model of light seemed to get clearer as he got nearer to it, the edges losing their shimmer. Details emerged. Devin could see the carousel now, and the tree houses and even the wretched ice-cream truck in its spot behind the long hedge. Penn left nothing to chance, he thought. Everything about the Home was planned, down to the last blade of grass.

He reached out and then stopped. What was it the boy had said? Something about a ball. He must need it to activate the model. He bent, grunting from the effort and peered underneath the table. Perhaps there was a drawer down there, hidden below.

Not a drawer but a small shelf. Resting on it was a white globe no larger than an egg. Devin reached for it, squeezing it slightly in the palm of his hand. At once numbers shimmered into view above the model, dozens and dozens of them, arranged in rows and columns. Devin's eyes locked onto them.

Then they vanished. The code was gone.

"Someone's been a very naughty boy," a voice said.

Devin whirled around. Mrs. Babbage was standing in the doorway.

Twenty-Four

"We can't allow you to look at that, now can we?" she said. "That wouldn't do at all."

There was another white ball in her hand. She tossed it into the air and caught it playfully.

"I knew you were faking," she said. "I saw you peeking, Devin dear."

Devin couldn't say anything. His voice was stuck in his throat.

Mrs. Babbage looked at him, her head tilted to one side as if she were about to tell him off for having his elbows on the table during lunch.

"I don't like to think what's going to happen to you now," she said. "But we can't have anyone knowing what really goes on here, can we?"

Devin didn't try to deny anything. He knew it was no use.

"I won't tell anyone," he said. "I mean it. I just want to get out."

Mrs. Babbage walked forward, her sandals making a slapping sound on the floorboards. The light from the model cast green shadows on her thin cheeks.

"No kid has ever woken up in here," she said. "I wonder what makes you so different."

She was only four feet away. Devin was a grown man, but he was old. He knew he could no more tackle her successfully than if he were a toddler.

"The Administrator doesn't have to find out," he said, although he could tell it was useless to plead with her.

"Her?" Mrs. Babbage's lips pursed up so tight her mouth disappeared.

It sounded, Devin thought, as if all the hatred in the world had been crammed into that single word.

"She does nothing," Mrs. Babbage continued, "except order people around. And since that father of hers showed up, she's been even worse. Nothing's good enough for her, and I've had enough of it."

She paused. An expression of cunning dawned over her features.

"Actually, it would serve her right if I didn't tell . . ."

She smiled, showing her small gray teeth. "Why should I? She's done nothing for me."

"That's right, you don't have to tell," Devin said.

Mrs. Babbage shot him a gleeful look. "I wouldn't get your hopes up, Devin, dear. I'll tell her all right, but only when I'm ready. Perhaps in front of that wonderful father of hers. She wants him to think she runs this place perfectly . . . Well, my news would show her up, wouldn't it? Pay her back for how she's treated me."

She took his arm. "You must be very tired," she murmured in his ear. "I think it's time you went back to your room for a nice little rest."

Devin let himself be led away.

✦ ✦ ✦

Someone was calling his name. A girl, her voice high and sharp.

"Devin!"

The word floated above him, rippling and distorted. He swam up toward it, his limbs heavy, his hands beating the darkness.

"Devin!"

He opened his eyes with a start. Kit was tugging on his arm as if she could physically drag him out of sleep. He was on his bed in his room at the Home; he was back from the Place. He turned his head and saw Malloy and Luke standing nearby.

"He's awake!" Malloy cried.

"You've been asleep for hours," Kit said. "What happened? Did you get the code?"

Devin sat up, bewildered. He shivered slightly.

"Did you get it?" Luke insisted.

"Give him a minute," Malloy chimed in. "He's still foggy."

Devin shook his head. "I'm okay . . . I looked for the code everywhere. I nearly got caught. It was hard . . . I couldn't hide, couldn't get down on my knees . . ."

"Okay," Luke said. "Take your time. Start from the beginning."

Devin drew a deep breath and told them what had happened. How he'd searched the offices and overheard the Administrator's meeting with the Visitors and found Gabriel Penn in a dream when he was still a small and trusting boy.

By the time he got to the part about the model of light and the little white ball, the others were on the edges of their seats with tension, and when he told them about the code appearing and then disappearing, they exploded.

"What?" Luke shouted.

Malloy covered his face with his hands.

"I can't believe it!" Luke cried. "If only you'd had more time!"

Devin stared at them in confusion.

"At least you tried, Devin," Kit said softly. "You tried your best."

"But . . . I saw it!" Devin said. "Didn't you hear me?" He drew in his breath sharply as understanding dawned.

They don't know what I can do. Until this moment, even I didn't know.

Kit had told him the way he saw things was like a secret power, and now he understood what she meant. It wasn't a power like X-ray vision or invisibility; it wasn't nearly as interesting or as incredible as that. But it had been exactly the power he'd needed when he came across the security codes for the Home.

"I can memorize things, complicated things," he said, his words tumbling out in a rush. "I can do it really, really fast. I didn't think it was anything special. But it is, isn't it? Remember how surprised you were, Luke, when I told you how many books there were in the Administrator's office? And the scavenger hunt—I knew where everything was without having to hunt like everyone else. And before that, in the city, I would never get lost, Kit, because I'd seen all the buildings from your rooftop. I had memorized them all. I only got a glimpse of the code for a few seconds, but it was enough."

Devin had to stop for breath. "The numbers were in the shape of a square," he continued more calmly. "Twelve columns of twelve numbers, 144 in total. The first column read 01, 33, 19, 02, . . ."

Luke scrambled for a piece of paper. "Hang on. Let me get a pen."

He wrote steadily while Devin dictated. At last he put down his pen.

"How did you remember all that?"

Devin felt embarrassed. "I don't know," he mumbled. "I can just do it. Numbers and letters, they make different sounds for me, and they're different colors too, so they stick in my mind. They kind of make a pattern . . . like a map. And then there are all the shapes in between the numbers—they make another pattern. And some of them I feel on my skin too . . ." His voice trailed off. "Don't you understand?"

Malloy was shaking his head. "No," he said. "We really, really don't, Strange Boy."

"It's like a page of words," Devin said, trying again. "If they were just random words, you'd never remember them, would you? But if the words made a story, it would stick in your head. I think that's how I remember things— because everything makes a kind of story for me."

There was a short silence. They still didn't understand, Devin thought. He couldn't explain it. But perhaps it didn't really matter.

"I thought you were a fool," Kit said. "I was so wrong."

Luke was staring at the piece of paper, gnawing on his lip. "Never mind about all that," he said. "I've got to think. You realize there are too many numbers here? You can't possibly have to enter each one of them to shut down the laser posts . . . unless it's a code."

"A code for a code?" Malloy piped up.

"Shut up! Let me think!" Luke tapped his pen against his knees, his eyes narrowing to slits. "Twelve columns . . . twelve numbers in each . . . twelve laser posts . . .

"Got it!" he said, sounding almost disappointed. "It's actually kind of lame. See if you can guess. What else has twelve?"

"Twelve eggs in a carton?" Malloy suggested.

"Oh, just tell us!" Kit snapped. "This isn't a math quiz, Luke."

"Twelve months in a year," Luke announced. "Look, the first number of the top row is 01. That's January. Next 02, that's obviously February. So the code changes every month. You don't have to enter all the numbers, just the ones in the column for that particular month. There's twelve numbers in every column, one for each of the twelve laser posts. Very simple."

"For a genius . . . ," Malloy said.

They all looked at each other. "So that's it. We've got everything." Kit said. "You figured out a diversion, Malloy?"

"I guess so."

"So when are we going to do it?"

"How about tomorrow? That gives us a little more time to plan," Luke said, his eyes starting to twitch.

"We can't wait," Devin said. "Mrs. Babbage said she wouldn't tell right away, but she's only waiting until she can humiliate the Administrator as much as possible. She might have told already. We have to go as soon as possible."

Kit looked at her watch. "It's now or never," she said. "I say we go during lunch."

✦ ✦ ✦

Kit told Devin to grab a backpack and fill it with things they might need later, once they were out. Warm clothes, a flashlight and penknife, any camping equipment he could find. Devin stood in his room after the others had left and tried to concentrate on the task.

In the two days he'd been away in the Dream, it had grown even hotter. Despite lavish watering, there was a brittle, dried-out quality to the plants in the courtyard. The leaves on the trees made a rasping, insect sound when the breeze stirred them, and the sun was small and pale, as though it had shriveled in its own heat.

Sweat prickled on his face despite the coolness of the room.

He grabbed his bag and started stuffing it as fast as he could.

The light had turned a pale, sickly yellow. It made the faces of the children in the dining room look drained of all blood. Kit, Luke, and Devin sat in front of their food, hardly speaking.

Caspar sat at the next table. He was working his way through a huge sandwich and looked a little healthier, although he was still wearing his suit.

I hope he can run in it, Devin thought.

"Get your stuff under the table!" Kit said, pushing her backpack out of sight. "Mrs. Babbage is coming!"

They did as they were told. Each had a bag except for Malloy. Luke was keeping Malloy's for him because he was busy. When Mrs. Babbage entered, Malloy was walking around the dining room, pausing by each table to whisper something to the kids sitting there. The instant he caught sight of Mrs. Babbage, he straightened up and put on his most innocent expression. But she wasn't looking at him. She made her way to the front of the room and clapped her hands for silence. She was staring straight at Devin, and when she caught his eye she gave him a tiny wink.

"Did you see that?" Kit whispered. "Has she told already? Is it too late?"

"I have an announcement," Mrs. Babbage said. "A lovely announcement!"

The room stilled.

"I have just heard from the Administrator that Megs, Jared, and Pavel have been adopted! They will be leaving for their new homes tomorrow. So all of you have plenty of time to say good-bye and wish them good luck with their new lives."

There was a scraping of chairs as the kids in the dining room rose to clap. Devin, Kit, and Luke rose with them. Out of the corner of his eye, Devin noticed Roman pushing his way toward the door; he looked quickly back at Mrs. Babbage. She was staring at Devin with a strange little smile on her face. He felt certain she was about to say something to him, but she walked right past and out of the dining room without another word.

As soon as she was gone, Malloy hurried over to their table. "I told everyone to hang around. Said there was going to be a show." He looked very nervous.

"Oh, God," Luke said. "You'd better have something good planned, Malloy. This has to work, it has to . . ."

"Stop it!" Kit said fiercely. "This is going to work and we're going to get out of here. But we've got to keep our heads and not panic. I know we can do it."

"What if you're chicken? What if you're more chicken than chicken soup?" Malloy said.

Kit gave him a long, hard look. "Then you pretend you're not. You pretend so hard it comes true."

Dessert had been laid out on the buffet table and kids were already helping themselves to it. "Okay, Malloy," Kit said. "You've got fifteen minutes, max. Can you be ready in fifteen minutes?"

Malloy paused, his eyes wide. Then he nodded.

"Remember where we're going to meet?"

"Hill outside, behind the maze and bushes."

"All right, then. Go!"

Malloy turned without another word and left the dining room.

Twenty-Five

THE MINUTES TICKED BY, five and then ten. Devin, Kit, and Luke sat in silence, not looking at each other.

"He's not going to be able to do it, is he?" Luke whispered in agitation.

Kit looked at her watch for the tenth time.

"It's been fifteen minutes already . . ."

"Shut up Luke! You're losing it."

The kids around them were finishing their dessert and starting to get up from their seats.

"He'll do it," Devin said. "I know he will."

Kit nodded, her lips tight.

There was a commotion at the window. Someone called out and kids were suddenly raising their heads to look. Devin heard a few gasps and then a muffled squeal of laughter.

"This is it!" Kit said, grabbing her bag. The dining room was abuzz with talk.

"I don't believe it!"

"You've gotta see this!"

"Is that animal driving a car?"

The doorway was jammed with kids all trying to get out at once. They spilled into the courtyard, pushing and shoving to get a better look. Kit, Luke, and Devin followed behind, keeping close to the building. For a few seconds they couldn't see anything, and then the crowd parted and they saw a red miniature car.

Malloy was in the passenger seat. He had raided the dress-up box and found himself a tuxedo and a shiny black top hat. He was grinning with terror. Fulsome was sitting next to him, hooves planted on the steering wheel of the car as if he were driving. Malloy had dressed him in a tiny white shirt with the top two buttons undone, and on his head, slightly askew, sat a dark, glossy wig.

The resemblance was unmistakable.

"It's her!" Karen whispered.

"Oh my goodness!" Caspar exclaimed.

The children stared in disbelief. Around and around the courtyard went the car, Malloy steering it with his left hand. From the corner of his eye, Devin saw staff members running toward the commotion.

"This will get her out," Kit said. "It has to."

But there was no sign of the Administrator. Kit, Luke,

and Devin eased their way behind the crowd, making for the door to the tower. Behind them, the car stopped in the center of the courtyard and Malloy got out. He stood uncertainly as if half paralyzed, then scuttled around to the other side of the car and opened the door.

"We have arrived, My Lady," he told Fulsome in a voice that was meant to be grand but came out in a frightened squeak. A ripple of laughter ran around the courtyard.

Fulsome descended. He ambled forward and then stopped to have a look around him. His wig had slipped even further, exposing a large pink ear, and his shirt was now missing several buttons. His stomach strained against the fabric and his thick front legs almost burst the seams of the arms.

But the pig had dignity, there was no denying it. If Fulsome was humiliated by his appearance, he gave no sign of it. He walked with his snout up, his tail perky, and his eyes alive for good things to eat. He was so gloriously proud that he made it look as if he wasn't dressed as the Administrator at all.

He made it look as if *she* were dressed like *him*.

"Good old Malloy," Luke muttered. "I'm sorry I doubted him."

"Seems to be a pattern with you . . . ," Kit said. But Devin could tell she only partly meant it. The three of them were close to the tower by now, keeping to the wall and moving slowly to avoid notice.

"Would you care for a stroll, My Lady?" Devin heard Malloy say. Mrs. Babbage had now joined the throng along with several more staff members. "Get that disgusting animal out of here!" her voice shrilled. There was a scuffle around the pig, and suddenly Fulsome had broken through and was charging around in the flower beds.

"You go, Pig!" somebody yelled. In a minute, twenty kids had taken up the cry.

"Go, Pig! Go, Pig! Go, Pig!"

Fulsome, excited by the attention, got up on his hind legs and turned on the spot. Vanessa forgot to be grown up and gave a hysterical cheer. Somebody grabbed Jared's teddy bear and flung it high into the air. The cries of the crowd became a roar.

GO-PIG! GO-PIG! GO-PIG! GO-PIG!

"Stop it at once," Mrs. Babbage said, apparently addressing Fulsome himself.

PIG! PIG! PIG!

Malloy stood in the middle of it all, waving his hands vaguely as if horrified by the ruckus he'd created. Mrs. Babbage turned to a pair of burly staff members. "Do something! Catch it or something!"

Kit, Luke, and Devin had reached the tower. They stayed around the side of it, keeping to the shadows.

"Why isn't she coming out?" Luke said. "This whole thing is pointless if she doesn't come out."

The two staff members had decided to use trickery to

catch Fulsome. Someone had fetched a large bread roll and was now waving it in the pig's direction. Fulsome stared at it thoughtfully. He took a couple of steps forward and sniffed.

"Don't do it!" a kid cried.

But Fulsome was not one to ignore any kind of food. He took another two steps. He was now almost within grabbing range of the man holding the bread.

"No-o-o-o," wailed the crowd.

The door of the tower banged open and suddenly the Administrator was there. Peering around the curved wall, Devin caught only a glimpse of her, her body rigid, her hands clenched into fists. For a second she stood there, perfectly still, and then, with terrifying speed, she moved.

When Fulsome had run loose before, the Administrator had thought Ansel was responsible. But she was not fooled now. Four or five swift strides brought her to her target. Her arm shot out and seized Malloy around the neck so tightly that his top hat fell off and his eyes bugged out.

A dreadful silence fell. The only sound was the gasping bark of Malloy trying to breathe.

Slowly, very deliberately, the Administrator bent her shining head as if to whisper something in Malloy's ear. But before she could say a word, she was interrupted by Mrs. Babbage, sounding full of panic.

"Visitors!"

She waved her arms frantically, pointing.

Devin looked out past the courtyard to the large meadow and the gates beyond. Five large cars had appeared in a line, moving up the driveway.

It was another group, eager for a tour of the Home. Business was certainly booming.

The cars were still distant, and they were moving very slowly in order not to jar the fragile, ancient bodies of their passengers. But in a very few minutes they would be pulling in to the courtyard. And then the Visitors would step out, not into the orderly paradise they were expecting, but into a scene of total chaos.

Exactly the same thought must have occurred to the Administrator. Her head shot up and, for a second, her whole body froze.

Then several things happened almost at once.

Malloy wriggled wildly and freed himself from the Administrator's grip. He leaped toward the miniature car, yelling for Fulsome. The pig halted in his tracks and then plunged after him, knocking a staff member to the ground. Mrs. Babbage screamed. Fulsome's wig flew off and several children made a dive for it.

Malloy jumped into the car and took off recklessly down the path toward the corn maze with Fulsome crammed in beside him. All the children immediately stampeded after them, followed by the members of staff.

In sixty seconds, the only people left in the courtyard were Mrs. Babbage and the Administrator. Kit, Luke, and Devin shrank against the wall of the tower. If the Administrator had turned, she would have seen them, but her attention was fixed on the convoy of cars, which was advancing steadily.

"What's she going to do?" Devin whispered.

"I bet she'll try to head them off," Kit said. "There's another place for cars to park behind the dining room. She'll try to redirect them there, then get them into the building quickly before they have a chance to see anything."

As they watched, the Administrator gathered herself. She straightened, flicked an invisible mark off the front of her shirt, and nodded to Mrs. Babbage, who scuttled off without another word. Then the Administrator began to walk—very fast but with no apparent haste—across the courtyard and down the driveway toward the approaching cars.

Kit grabbed her bag. "Now's our chance. Come on."

The three of them made a dash for the tower door.

✦ ✦ ✦

"Can we lock it?" Kit panted, slamming it closed.

Luke fumbled with the handle. "Not sure . . ."

"Never mind, then, leave it. Get in the elevator."

Luke punched the button for the top floor. They crowded together, perfectly still, their bodies tight with tension, their faces looking desperately white in the elevator light's glow. In the few seconds of silence as the elevator rose, they heard a soft, whimpering, scratching sound, very close. Luke's whole body jerked.

"It's just Frisker," Kit said, patting her backpack. "You don't think I'd leave this place without Frisker, do you?"

The elevator hissed and the door slid open and the Administrator's office was laid out before them.

Kit put her bag down carefully on the floor and rummaged in her pocket for the key to the control box. She pulled it out and tossed it to Luke.

"It's up to you now," she said.

Luke was at the Administrator's desk. "There's a button here somewhere that opens the panel hiding the control box . . . I saw her press it . . . ah, here it is."

A small rectangle slid open on the wall of fake books.

Luke had unlocked the control box and was hunched over a sheet of glass. Small lights were blinking on the surface in an apparently random pattern, but Luke didn't seem disturbed by this. In fact he looked calmer than he had in days. He rubbed his hands together.

"Pretty basic stuff," he murmured. "It uses touch recognition but there's an easy way around that . . ."

Kit and Devin clustered around him, watching. His fingers flew over the glass, swiping and tapping. The small lights began to form a line. "I thought so," Luke muttered. "It's completely predictable. You'd think they would have installed something a bit more advanced."

"Just get on with it," Kit said. "You need the code yet?"

"In a minute. Okay . . . I'm in. Give me the numbers."

Kit pulled out the piece of paper with the code and began dictating to Luke. His fingers hesitated. His eyes scanned the screen anxiously.

"What's the matter?"

"Slight glitch. I can enter the numbers but I don't know which laser posts they correspond to. I could find out but it's going to take me a couple more minutes."

"Does it matter? Just put them all in. Then all the posts will go down."

"Okay, keep going."

Kit continued to read the numbers aloud, and this time Luke's fingers flew across the glass panel. "That's one out . . . that's two . . . that's three . . ."

Frisker whimpered again in Kit's bag and made a scrabbling noise as he tried to get out. Kit hesitated, the paper shaking slightly in her hand.

"That's four out," Luke said. "Eight to go. We'll be out of here in—"

He was interrupted by a piercing noise, half whistle, half roar. Devin's hands shot up to cover his ears.

"Security alarm!" Luke shouted.

"What did you do?" Kit was yelling herself.

"Nothing! Someone else must have set it off." He

banged at the glass panel with his fist. "I can't go on. It's overriding everything."

"You have to!" Kit screamed. "Try!" The alarm had risen to an earsplitting shriek.

"It's no good!"

Devin ran to the window that overlooked the court-yard. The alarm suddenly stopped. In the silence he heard Luke's voice, babbling in panic.

"We've got four down, but which four? Which ones? There's no way to tell."

"I don't think it matters anymore," Devin said quietly. "Take a look at this."

Far below they saw a crowd of people: the children and all the staff members and Mrs. Babbage, her thin hair out of its bun and hanging in disheveled strands. The Visitors who had arrived in the convoy of cars were standing to one side in a huddle, looking completely bewildered. In front of them all, the Administrator stood, her hands on her hips. Even from this distance she looked terrifying.

Everyone's head was turned in exactly the same direction.

They were all looking up at the top of the tower.

Twenty-Six

KIT, LUKE, AND DEVIN shrank down, away from the window.

"What did we do to set off the alarm?" Kit whispered, her back to the wall.

Luke shook his head. "No, I told you, I don't think it was us. I was careful. I know how these systems work. Something else must have happened."

Devin raised himself and peered out the window again. "They're still there, just looking."

"How can they see us?" Kit said again.

"I'm not sure it's us they're looking at," Devin said, staring down. It seemed to him that the gaze of the crowd wasn't fixed on their window, but at a point somewhere above them. "I think they're looking at something else."

"It doesn't matter," Kit said. "We're still trapped

aren't we? The minute we walk out of here, they'll see us. Even if they didn't, we don't know which posts are down and which are still active. We don't know what direction to run in." Her fists clenched. "She's not going to get me again. I'll trash this place before I let her get me again."

Devin had risen to his feet and was levering the window upward. The casing was a little stiff, and he had to shove hard. Luke made a grab for him. "What are you doing? They'll see you!"

But Devin had the window open and was leaning out. Immediately, the eyes of the crowd below turned in his direction. Then they turned back to a spot just above him. Devin leaned out farther, craning his neck, trying to see what they were looking at. The top of the tower was about twenty feet above him, invisible from this angle. Before the others could stop him, he scrambled out through the window onto the broad ledge, turning and inching sideways.

He knew better than to look down. He shuffled along the window ledge until he came to the end of it. The wall of the tower was irregular here, with several large chunks of masonry missing. If he judged it just right, he could find enough footholds to climb to the top of the window, which jutted out far enough to provide a perch for him. He put out a foot, found a crack in the wall, and hauled himself up, his hands scrabbling to hold on.

Below him, he heard Kit calling to him, but he couldn't make out the words.

The wind was stronger up here than he thought it would be, a harsh white roar in his throat, tugging at his insides and battering his body. His jacket blew up and whipped at his shoulders with a sound that was half a shout and half a scream. He sucked in his breath, found another foothold, and swung upward again. Three more feet and he would be at the relative safety of the perch. His hand was slippery; he tried to wipe it against his shirt, found himself off balance, and for one terrible moment felt himself about to fall. Somehow, he clung on, face crammed against the sandy stone, heart hammering, too frightened to continue but equally certain he could never make it back.

His grandfather's voice was a whisper in his ear.

Try again, Dev, try again, my lad.

Devin's foot found the next step. His arm reached out and grasped the perch, and he heaved himself up and lay there panting. Then he stood up carefully. The roof of the tower was still a good ten feet above him, and he could see that he had no chance of climbing any farther; from that point on, the wall was perfectly smooth, without a single foot- or handhold. But now that he was higher, he saw what everyone below was staring at so intently.

It was Roman. Devin remembered how he'd slipped from the dining room after Mrs. Babbage had made her announcement. He must have been climbing the tower while Malloy was still running around the courtyard with Fulsome.

Roman was standing on the edge of the roof. Heat haze blurred his outline, making his body shimmer and appear to sway. But his face was as fixed as stone.

Devin looked back down at the courtyard. Nobody had moved. They were all still staring up. From this distance, their faces were nothing but pale smudges.

He shuffled to the edge of his perch. "Roman!"

The boy glanced down at him without expression, as though he had reached a place beyond recognition or even surprise. He looked away.

"Roman! What are you doing?"

The wind blew Roman's shirt tight against his body. He took another step forward. He was almost at the very edge of the roof now.

"Don't!" Devin cried, reaching one arm hopelessly toward him. "Don't!"

Below him on the ground, many of the children covered their faces with their hands. Someone had left and come back with a megaphone and was shouting something into it. But the words were lost on the wind. Devin looked back at Roman.

"*Why?*" Devin asked.

But even before the word was out of his mouth, he knew.

"It's because of Megs isn't it?" he said. "It's all because of Megs. You didn't do any of this to protect yourself, or for money. You did it for Megs."

Roman lowered his head and looked down at Devin, as if for the first time. His eyes had a bruised appearance, like he'd been grinding his fists against them. "We arrived here together, over a year ago," he said in a dull voice. "She reminded me of . . ." He paused, unable to speak for a second or two.

"I had a little sister once, but I lost her. In a flash flood behind our house after a storm. I was holding on to her but she . . . she slipped through my fingers. I saw her face before she went under. She was crying out for me." He lifted his right hand and stared at it. "I had hold of her . . ."

Devin remembered the conversation he'd overheard the night of the campout. "You couldn't save her but you thought you could save Megs."

"Megs was normal when I met her. Just a sweet, normal little girl. But they changed her. I saw her getting disturbed . . . all the fire stuff . . . I couldn't stand to see it. I promised myself I wouldn't lose her like I lost my sister."

"The Administrator told you Megs wouldn't have to go to the Place anymore if you went out and found more children."

A terrible resignation spread over Roman's face.

"Yeah. But I didn't find enough kids. She said I wasn't useful to her anymore. I should have known she'd break her promise.

"They'll dump her back on the streets," Roman said, as if talking to himself. "And she'll die. All by herself in a corner somewhere."

"No," Devin said, "she won't if—"

But Roman wasn't listening to him any longer. His right foot had crept over the edge of the roof. "I'm a traitor," he muttered. "But I wasn't like that before, I wasn't that person . . ."

"You're still not," Devin said. "It's not too late."

Roman shook his head.

"We need you," Devin pleaded. A sudden gust of wind caught him and pinned him to the side of the tower. He waited for it to pass, his cheek pressed tight against the stone, his mind groping for the right thing to say.

"You were on a baseball team," he said. "You were the catcher," he said.

He didn't wait for Roman to reply but carried on, his words tumbling out. "Luke's in the office, he's disabled four of the laser posts but we don't know which ones. If we run the wrong way we'll be caught. You said that from where the catcher stands he can see the whole field. Do you remember that, Roman?"

The boy swayed slightly on the lip of the roof.

"We need you, Roman," Devin said softly. "We need you to be the catcher again."

Roman's lips tightened.

"Where are they? Can you see?"

Roman seemed to shudder and his shoulders dropped. He stepped back.

"Yes," he said. "I can see them all. Most of them still have their lights flashing. But the ones behind the farm-yard and the meadow—those are out."

"You sure?"

He nodded. "You should head over there."

"Thanks, Roman, thank you . . ."

"Wait. You'll never get past that crowd in the court-yard." There were several loose bricks scattered over the roof of the tower and Roman bent and picked one up. "I told you the catcher's got a lightning arm," he said grimly. "Watch this."

He leaned back slightly, his shoulder curving into a long, smooth swing, and flung the brick into the court-yard. Devin heard cries of alarm, saw children scattering. Roman bent and got another brick. "I'll get her with this one," he said. He aimed and sent it hurtling down. Devin watched it fly straight at the Administrator, stand-ing motionless below.

"It hit the ground right next to her!" Devin cried.

The Administrator was stumbling backward. An-other brick was already in Roman's hand. His body was steady, his face full of concentration. The brick sailed toward Mrs. Babbage, who gave a thin scream and bolted for the shelter of the dining room. Staff members jumped to hustle the old folks away.

"You'd better hurry," Roman shouted. "I can't hold them off forever. Once I'm out of bricks, they'll be back."

"What about you?"

"I'll manage. Get out of here!"

Another brick went whistling through the air. Devin ducked his head and scrambled down the footholds to the window ledge below. He slid through the window feet first.

"It's clear behind the farmyard," he panted. "Roman's on the roof, he could see. He's keeping the crowd away, but we don't have much time."

They grabbed their bags and bolted toward the elevator. Outside, the courtyard was completely empty. The Administrator couldn't have been far away, Devin thought, but nobody dared to brave the open with Roman still on the roof hurling his missiles. As if to prove his point, a brick slammed down and hit the ground twenty feet from where they stood.

"Come on!" They took off running toward the farmyard.

"Get the others!" Devin cried. "Tell everyone you see . . ."

Kit was ahead, her braid bouncing against her back as she raced.

The rest of the children were in a bewildered group behind the buildings on the far side of the courtyard. The minute they caught sight of Kit and the others, they rushed forward.

"What happened to Roman?"

"Is the Administrator dead?"

"Where are you going?"

"Come with us! Just run!" Kit yelled. "We'll explain later . . . Everyone's gotta get out of here!"

They moved off in a herd, running as fast as they could, Jared still clutching his teddy bear, Karen whimpering as she tried to keep up, Caspar trotting along stiffly, Pavel silent, as always.

Devin peeled off to the side. "Devin!" Kit shouted. "Where are you going?"

"The mare," Devin said, "I want to get the mare."

"It's the wrong direction!"

But Devin had already turned and was racing toward the large field. Kit hesitated and then handed her backpack with Frisker inside to Missie and ran after Devin. It was a good quarter of a mile down the long driveway to the horse's gate, but they didn't see anyone as they flew along, side by side. Then, from the corner of his eye, Devin saw the cars of the Visitors turning down the smaller driveway on the other side of the Home. They were heading for the exit, he thought, leaving in a hurry. For a second he imagined the Administrator's utter fury and he stumbled slightly. Kit caught his arm.

"You're crazy, you know that?" she panted. "We could be out of here by now."

They reached the gate and Devin flung it open. From the other side of the field, the mare lifted her head. "Here," Devin called to her. "Here, to me . . ."

She came at a trot, her face eager. Devin reached for her neck as she turned, prancing a little with excitement. She was missing her bridle, but it didn't matter. He grabbed her mane and swung himself up onto her back, leaning down for Kit.

"I can't," Kit said, her face twisting in fear, "I don't know how."

"It's okay," Devin said. "It's easy, I've got you." He grabbed her under her arm and pulled her up, her legs scrambling and slipping against the side of the horse.

"Hold on," he said.

"Wait! Devin stop! Devin! "

The mare broke into a canter. Devin heard the lovely chestnut sound of her shoes striking the gravel of the driveway. "Hold on!" he cried again. Kit jolted wildly behind him, but then she steadied and found her balance.

"Go around," she said in his ear. "There'll be people in the courtyard, go around by the pool."

They had to slow down among the trees but instantly picked up speed again once they reached the path by the swimming pool. At a small fork, Devin came to a stop. He caught a glimpse of four or five staff members coming at a run on their right, and Devin automatically turned the horse left.

They were at the head of the path leading to the Place. Devin hesitated and then urged the mare on at a walk. From his high vantage point, the twisted trees looked smaller and the way less dark, but there was still a memory of terror in those knotted depths. Neither Devin nor Kit spoke, and even the hooves of the mare fell silent on the shadowed path.

They reached the clearing at last and stopped.

The Administrator was standing in the doorway of the Place, twenty feet away. Roman was there too. She had his left arm pinned against his back. His right arm dangled, horribly bent and crooked. The bone was shattered; Devin had seen enough animals with broken limbs to recognize that immediately. But perhaps more terrible than this was the sight of the Administrator's hand closed in a tight grip around the injured arm. Roman was strong and almost as tall as she was, but he wasn't struggling. Even the smallest movement must cause him agony.

The Administrator's head whipped around.

"Stop right there," she told Devin.

"What have you done to him?" Kit cried.

"Nothing," she said. "I found him like this."

"He'll never throw again," she added with satisfaction.

Devin suddenly noticed Darwin. The bird was clinging by one claw to the Administrator's back. He must have been dislodged from her shoulder in the struggle with Roman.

"Get down off the horse," the Administrator ordered. "All I have to do is give the signal and twenty staff members will be here. You'll be sorry if they have to take you by force."

"You can't stop us," Kit cried in a high voice. "We'll run you over!"

The Administrator's expression changed. It became conspiratorial, almost friendly.

"Kit," she said smoothly, "I believe I underestimated you."

"Yeah," Kit said. "A lot of people make that mistake."

"I knew you were different from the others when you arrived," the Administrator said, her voice calm, her eyes never leaving Kit's face. "But I must confess I didn't understand you."

"You said I was damaged!" Kit burst out.

"Don't talk to her," Devin said. "Don't listen . . ."

"Then, when you stole my key—I didn't notice until far too late, by the way—I realized what sort of person you are. Someone who does what it takes to get what they want and who succeeds at it." She paused. "We're alike that way, you and I."

"That's not true!" Devin burst out. "She's nothing like you!"

"All your friends may have escaped," the Administrator continued, ignoring him. "But it hardly matters. Most of them had become useless anyway. I shall simply find new children. You could help me run this place, Kit. Together we could make it even better than before."

"What about Mrs. Babbage?" Kit said.

"Mrs. Babbage is packing her bags. She was a servant, a nothing, a sniveler who ran away at the first sign of trouble. With you it would be different. You could find the children. Roman was very unsatisfactory in the job. His heart was never in it. But I know they'd trust you. You'd be a great success. Then later, when you're older, you can have a full partnership in the business. Think about it."

Kit said nothing. In the silence, Devin heard Darwin give a muffled croak. He had regained his perch on the Administrator's shoulder and was settled in hunched obedience, his eyes closed to slits.

"I know what you dream of, Kit," the Administrator said. "This place makes more money than you can ever imagine. You'd have everything you've ever wanted."

Behind him on the horse, Devin felt Kit grow very still.

"You're right," Kit said.

Devin twisted, trying to face her, struggling to understand. "Kit!" he whispered. "Kit!"

"We are alike," Kit said. "We both have disgusting, rotten fathers."

The Administrator jerked as if she'd been shot.

"How dare you?" she said in a voice so thick with loathing that Devin could taste it like vomit in the back of his throat. "How dare you?"

"The difference is," Kit continued, "I got away from mine. Which makes me the opposite of you. So thanks for the offer, but I'd rather die."

"How dare you?" The Administrator repeated, as though unable to form any other words. "Get down from the horse and get inside now!"

"Or what?" Kit said.

The Administrator squeezed Roman's arm so tightly he cried out and his legs buckled.

"Or I'll break his other arm."

Looking at her face, Devin was certain she meant it.

"I want this place back up and running. Fresh kids, tighter rules, a new standard of excellence . . ." On her shoulder Darwin shifted uncomfortably, interrupting her flow of talk.

"Disgusting creature!" she cried in a shrill voice, batting at him with a furious sweep of her hand. Devin couldn't account for what happened next. Perhaps Darwin was spooked by the Administrator's rage. Perhaps he saw something in the twisted trees that frightened him. Or perhaps (as Malloy would later claim), being the most intelligent of all parrots, he understood human language better than anyone had thought.

Whatever the reason, he lunged at the Administrator's face in a furious clump of wings and feathers and stabbing beak. She cried out and threw up her hands, but the bird continued to attack as though making up for the long years behind bars, for all the darkness and the scorn and the neglect.

Roman, freed from the Administrator's grasp, fell forward onto his knees, then staggered to his feet, his broken arm pressed to his side.

"Can you run?" Devin shouted to him. "Get to the farmyard—we'll meet you on the other side!"

The parrot was circling above the Administrator's head now, beating the air with awkward, heavy wings. For a moment it flapped and struggled, fighting to keep airborne. Then it righted itself and, with a flick of its tail, soared above their heads.

"Bye-bye!" Darwin screamed.

"Go!" Kit yelled in Devin's ear. Devin looked for Roman and saw he'd gone. The Administrator was still cowering, her hands covering her face. Devin dug in his heels and they took off down the narrow path on the far side of the clearing, the mare's hooves raising great clouds of dust. They reached the entrance to the corn maze and plunged inside. Devin led the mare through it unhesitatingly, Kit clinging to him, gasping as the stalks whipped at her legs.

They reached the farmyard at last, and the bushes beyond it, and saw the outline of the nearest laser post.

Between the distant trees Devin saw a flash of bright red and heard the tooting of a horn.

"It's Malloy in the car!" Kit shouted. "They're through! It's safe!"

✦ ✦ ✦

The whole group had gathered together on top of the hill just beyond the perimeter. Almost all the kids were there. After a few minutes, they saw Roman coming toward them. He was stumbling and pale, but his head was held high.

Like a catcher, Devin thought, after a game hard won.

"You okay?" Devin asked him.

Roman slumped to the ground, panting. "I will be," he said, grimacing with pain.

"We've got to get a splint on that arm . . . It looks bad."

"In a minute, okay? Just need to catch my breath."

Devin sat down beside him. He gazed down at the buildings of the Home.

"Back on the tower," Devin said, "you could have hit her with that brick. You could have killed her if you'd wanted to."

"Probably."

"Why didn't you?"

"She made me into someone I wasn't once already," Roman said. "I wasn't going to let her do it twice."

"She'll just start again with new kids. She said she would. Nothing's stopping her is it?"

"Maybe, maybe not."

Devin stared at the buildings. Something was different. "The birds are gone," he said.

Then as he watched, he saw a flicker at the window of one of the buildings. It came again, a yellow streak that darted out, retreated, then appeared once more. A second streak appeared, as red as breath, and into Devin's mind came a trembling, sighing sound that ran like fingers down the back of his neck. A thin plume of smoke rose in a wavering column. He heard the small sound of glass breaking at a distance, and suddenly the window of the building was alive with flame.

"Megs," Roman said. "Before I went up onto the tower I gave her my lighter. I never saw her look so happy."

The other children had caught sight of the fire and stood open mouthed, watching as flames swirled furiously above the roofs and licked the walls of the Home. Then up the hill came a small figure. Her bow was gone and her cheeks were covered in soot. Roman held out his good hand.

"Give it back now, Megs."

She hesitated and then placed the lighter in his palm.

"You did good, but never again, you understand? It's done, it's over."

She nodded, very solemn. "Will everything be gone, Roman? Will all of it burn clean away?"

"Look how fast it's taking hold," Kit said. "It's been so dry, no rain for ages. I don't think there'll be as much as a pile of sticks left by morning." She was standing next to the mare as she spoke, stroking the animal's neck, her fear gone now. She turned to Devin.

"I still can't believe you stole her. I thought I was the best thief in the world, but she's better than anything I ever took."

"What do we do now?" somebody said.

"I'm hungry," Missie whined. "I didn't have any lunch. Did it occur to anyone to bring food?"

She looked at the motley group of kids: Malloy with an arm around Fulsome's neck, Jared and Vanessa and Karen disheveled and silent, Caspar with his mouth agape, Luke pacing and gnawing on his lip.

"I didn't think so," she said.

"We should get away from here," Luke said. "I don't want to get blamed for burning that place down."

Kit hoisted her pack onto her back. "Nor me. Come on, Frisker."

"Where are you going?" Malloy said.

Kit shrugged. "Back to the city, of course. You coming?

"I can't go to the city," Malloy wailed. "Fulsome will get eaten."

Luke stopped pacing. "Let's be honest, we don't have much of a choice."

"There's nowhere else to go," Karen whispered.

"The city again." Caspar's shoulders sagged. "I'm going to need a new suit, aren't I? Where am I going to find a new suit?"

Roman shook his head in weary disgust. One of the younger children started to snuffle and then cry.

"We could go to the farm," Devin said. His hand tightened on the mare's mane.

"All of us could. And the mare and Fulsome. I left because it was too much for one person, but together we could get it running again."

Nobody said anything.

"Maybe we'd find the cow, and the chickens that are left can't be far away," Devin continued, his words quickening with excitement. "And Glancer might still be there . . . There's a stream and a barn and a place to grow vegetables and you can catch rabbits. But best of all, it's not as hot there. The hills protect it . . ." His voice trailed off. The others were staring at him doubtfully.

"Sounds made-up," Missie announced.

"Yeah, kind of hard to believe, Strange Boy," Malloy added.

Devin shook his head. "No. What happened to us here is what's hard to believe. Life in the city is what's hard to believe. My granddad was right. At the farm all you have to worry about are ordinary things."

He glanced at Kit. "There isn't anywhere else like it. It's . . . it's a true rary."

She hesitated, her face full of doubt and hope.

"You won't have to gather stuff anymore because everything you need is right there," Devin told her, his voice soft. "It's the one safe place, Kit."

She looked at him with troubled eyes, and for a second he thought she would walk away. Then her shoulders relaxed.

"Sounds like something I should try, then." She turned to the others. "Who's in?"

"Me!" Malloy said, "Fulsome likes the whole idea."

Luke nodded, considering. "It's a plan . . ."

Everyone was suddenly talking at once.

"Will we plant seeds?" Caspar inquired. "Will we chop wood? I suspect I'll be excellent at chopping wood."

"I hope we find the chickens," Karen murmured. "I think I'd like chickens."

Devin listened to them talk, his mind ranging ahead. It would be a very long walk, and they'd have to keep out of sight, avoiding roads. We came from the west, he thought, then we turned southwest . . . Through the window of the car he'd seen hills that thudded yellow-soft, one after the other in a long line. Devin lifted his hand and tapped out their rhythm against the mare's warm neck until he was sure of the tune. That was the way they should go.

ACKNOWLEDGMENTS

With special thanks too my friends Bonnie Tenneriello and Andrew Sofer for their incredibly clever advice, my niece Isobel Jones and her support and enthusiasm, and my husband, David, for his unfaltering love. Thanks also to Elise Howard, whose editing made all the difference, and Rebecca Carter, the best agent in the world.

PROLOGUE

The yacht was as grand and as white as a wedding cake, and it was named *Everlasting*. Every inch of it had been polished, from the great, gleaming hull down to the last brass button on the uniforms of the three crewmen standing in line on deck. The anchor had been lifted and the vessel was ready for departure. But first there was a picture to be taken.

When you are as rich and as good-looking as the Fitzjohn family was, there is always someone who wants to take your picture.

The photographer from the society pages of the newspaper had arranged them on the dock with their yacht in the background. Or rather, he had *suggested* they pose that way, his smile very ingratiating because, after all, it was they who were doing him the favor.

There they stood under the bluest of all blue skies.

Mrs. Fitzjohn, her lovely face smiling under a large-brimmed, fashionable hat, and Mr. Fitzjohn, tanned and gallant in his navy blazer, gazing fondly at his wife. In front of them, their children, Marcus and Caroline. At seventeen, Marcus was almost as tall as his father and just as handsome. Caroline was six. She was holding a doll. The doll was also called Caroline. It had been handmade in Switzerland especially for her. It had the same color hair and eyes as her and was wearing the same yellow cotton dress and yellow shoes that Caroline herself was wearing.

"Wonderful . . . lovely," the photographer said automatically as he fiddled with his camera. "Won't take a minute!" But then he looked—really *looked*—at them, and the breath suddenly caught in his throat.

It seemed that the Fitzjohn family were shining almost as brightly as the sunlight on the water of the bay. It wasn't just their wealth, the fact that along with the fabulous yacht, they owned a fleet of cars and a large, beautiful mansion called Brightwood Hall. Nor was it merely their good looks and glamour. Plenty of celebrities had these qualities, as he well knew.

No, he thought. It was happiness they shone with. The photographer had witnessed too many fake smiles not to recognize the real thing when he saw it. In that moment—that perfect moment—he thought the Fitzjohns looked like the happiest people in the entire world.

He sighed. The camera clicked.

"All done, Mr. Fitzjohn! Hope you have a great day on the water!"

Caroline Fitzjohn trotted after the others as they went on board. Daddy and Marcus would go straight to the pilot's deck like they always did, but Mummy had said there were cookies for her in the main cabin.

"We shall have tea!" she had said. "You and I and Dolly Caroline. Would you like that?"

Caroline thought she would like it very much, but now Mummy had disappeared somewhere. Perhaps she had gone to the pilot's deck after all, or perhaps she was in the bathroom.

Caroline stood in the main cabin waiting for her to come back and feeling lonely. But of course she wasn't really alone. She had Dolly Caroline with her. She stroked the doll's hair and straightened her dress.

"Oh, *Caroline,*" she said out loud. "You lost your shoe!"

For a moment she thought of calling out to her mother. But then she remembered that she was six years old. Six was old enough to look after her own things. Besides, she'd already realized where the shoe must have fallen off. She had been playing on a bench by the dock. The bench wasn't far away. She could see it through the cabin window.

It took only a minute to slip off the boat and run down the gangplank. And then she was on her hands and knees looking under the bench for the shoe. She couldn't see it anywhere, and then there it was, a scrap of yellow leather wedged between the wall and the back of the bench. Caroline climbed onto the seat and reached her arm down as far as it would go. She could feel the shoe! She scissored her fingers and tried to snag it, fearful that she would wedge it down

But she had a grip on it now, one finger hooked ...ay laces. She was pulling it to safety.

...omething made her look up. A premonition.

For a second, she saw only the large empty space where *Everlasting* had been. Then her gaze lifted, and she saw the yacht out in the bay. It was moving fast, there was white water behind it; the flag on its topmost mast was flattened to a sheet. Caroline ran to the edge of the dock.

The yacht was flying away. Two hundred yards, now three. She held Dolly Caroline tight to her chest and watched it go.

They had left without her. They hadn't known.

The driver, Mr. Hadley, came to pick her up. Her grandmother, who had stayed behind at home, would look after her for the day. Her family would be back that afternoon. Someone would radio the yacht to tell them she was safe. Mr. Hadley explained all this as he drove the twenty or so miles back to Brightwood Hall.

She sat in the back of the big car, gazing out of the window. She had always loved the sea, but now it suddenly seemed a featureless, unfriendly place. And there, far away, in the middle of the emptiness, looking no larger than a glittering brooch pinned to the very edge of the horizon, she saw *Everlasting*. She pressed her hand to the window, staring desperately. There was a bend in the road and then the yacht was gone.

"You'll take plenty of other trips," Mr. Hadley said. His voice was kinder than ever. "It's still only the start of summer."

But there were no more trips.